RETURN TO ROSEWOOD BEACH

ROSEWOOD BEACH BOOK ONE

FIONA BAKER

D1522691

Published in the United States of America

First Edition, 2025

fionabakerauthor.com

JOIN MY NEWSLETTER

If you love beachy, feel-good women's fiction, sign up to receive my newsletter, where you'll get free books, exclusive bonus content, and info on my new releases and sales!

CHAPTER ONE

Julia Owens stood in front of the full-length mirror in her New York apartment and turned slowly back and forth, inspecting her reflection. Early morning sunlight streamed across the floorboards of her chic bedroom, glinting on the glossy sheen of her toenail polish.

"No, that's not right either," she murmured, frowning a little as she looked at the emerald-green blazer that she'd paired with a black pencil skirt. She didn't want to look like she was asking for attention, and the green was too bright, she decided. But the skirt looked good, and she could pair it with the black heels she'd bought yesterday.

She took a deep breath, smiling a little to herself. A nervous, tingling kind of excitement was pulsing through her—it was that same excitement that had woken her up at five-thirty in the morning and prevented her from going back to sleep.

She glanced at the clock. It was now six-fifteen, and she'd been spending a little over half an hour trying to decide on her outfit for the day. She wanted to look and feel her best—and give off all the right signals—before the meeting later that morning. It was very important that she settled on an outfit that looked just right.

As she started to take off the blazer, a yawn overpowered her. She blinked, telling herself that she should go into the kitchen and start making some coffee.

I should have gotten more sleep before this big meeting, she thought, tucking the blazer back inside her perfectly organized, color-coded closet. *But I'm just too jittery.*

She smiled as she pulled a white blouse with a fancy collar out of her closet. She was going to do exceptionally well today, she felt sure of it. The last time the advertising firm she worked for had taken on a new client, they'd had the advertising event in Los Angeles, and she'd headed it up. That new client had been an organic dog food company, and Julia had done a fantastic job at the event.

She closed her eyes, focusing on remembering that day as a means of bolstering her confidence. She remembered the way she'd spoken to the representatives from the dog food company, and the positive way they'd responded—

She frowned for a moment, remembering some strange tension that had happened between her and her coworkers that day, but in the next moment, she brushed that memory aside. Emotions were always high during big events, and it wasn't something she should worry about. That partnership with the organic dog food company had been a success, and she figured that all's well that ends well.

She opened her eyes again and finished putting on the blouse. It was made of satin, and it was pleasantly soft to the touch.

"There." She grinned at her reflection, turning back and forth and inspecting herself. "That's it. I look like I'm ready to take on the whole world of advertising."

Once her outfit was decided on, she got back into her pajamas, since she didn't want to get her clothes wrinkly. She still had a lot of time before she needed to leave for the office, and she wanted to make herself a healthy breakfast and do her makeup carefully.

She went into the kitchen and started a pot of

coffee brewing. She used a gourmet coffee that she'd bought out in Los Angeles at an adorable little tea and coffee shop, and the air was soon filled with the rich, nutty aroma of the brewing beverage.

She prepared a banana mango smoothie for herself, along with a fried egg sandwich with avocado and tomato. She wanted to make sure she ate enough to give herself the mental energy she would need, especially since she hadn't gotten as much sleep as she should have.

She was used to planning all the details of her life carefully, the way she was planning that morning carefully. Ever since she'd graduated from college, she'd been determined to be successful in her advertising career. She'd worked hard and calculated all of her decisions with precision, making sure she always came out on top.

She ate her breakfast as she checked her emails and jotted down notes in her planner. The food was delicious, but she was focused more on her work than tasting it. When she'd finished, she went into her bathroom and started to carefully do her makeup and hair. It took her half an hour, and as she worked, she practiced how she would introduce herself to her firm's new potential partners by speaking into the mirror.

The new potential client was Cutie Pie, a baby product company, and it was a huge organization—it had the ability to skyrocket her company to greater heights if everything went well and Cutie Pie signed on to do business with them. She felt eager to take on the challenge of making sure she and her coworkers made an excellent impression on Cutie Pie. She'd already studied their products in great detail—something she'd done as soon as she'd heard they might be signing on. Although she didn't have any kids of her own and she wasn't particular familiar with baby products, she'd done her research and she already had a lot of great ideas for advertisements. She'd always been great at coming up with innovative ideas, even for products she didn't use.

She finished her makeup and stepped back from the mirror, smiling in approval over her appearance. She gave herself a brisk nod, feeling that she was ready at last for her big day. She got dressed into her work clothes, and just before leaving her apartment, she grabbed a chic black raincoat to throw on—it was early April, and still often cold and rainy.

She made her way through downtown New York City to the skyscraper where her advertising firm, Caldunski Inc., had their offices. Her heels clicked across the cement as she hurried up to the glass front doors. She stepped inside and was greeted by the feeling of cool air on her face and the familiar smell of the downstairs lobby, which always had a lingering aroma of patchouli.

She took the elevator up to her floor, adjusting her bracelets and giving herself an internal pep talk. She checked her reflection in the elevator mirror, making sure that the up-do she'd created with her long brown hair was still smooth. Her sharp, well-defined features looked particularly attractive because of the way she'd done her makeup, and she felt her confidence surge.

She stepped out of the elevator and made her way toward the meeting room. She'd arrived before the meeting was due to start, but she saw no harm in sitting down at the table a little early. Punctuality looked professional. She put on a confident smile as she strode toward the meeting room, even though her heart was fluttering a little bit with nervousness.

"Hey, Julia?"

Julia turned and saw the firm's secretary, Kenzie, hurrying toward her with a worried expression.

"Good morning, Kenzie." She smiled cheerfully at the other woman. "You look great," she added, admiring Kenzie's bright pink blazer, although she was glad she herself hadn't worn anything that flashy. Secretaries could wear whatever they wanted, really—she needed to make a more professional impression than that.

"Thanks," Kenzie stammered, looking a little uncomfortable.

"Is everything okay?" Julia frowned, curious as to why Kenzie was acting so oddly.

"Has Marshall talked to you yet?"

Julia shook her head, feeling a sudden sense of foreboding in her stomach. "No, he hasn't. Not today. Why?"

At that moment, their boss, Marshall, stepped out of his office and nodded at Julia. The look on his face was somewhat grim, and the sloshy feeling in Julia's stomach intensified.

"Come on into my office for a minute, Julia," he said, not quite making eye contact with her.

"Um, okay." She turned to Kenzie, wondering what was going on, but the secretary avoided eye contact with her as well.

Straightening her shoulders, Julia followed Marshall inside his office. He gestured for her to take a seat in the chair placed on the opposite of his desk, and she sat down, trying not to squirm.

"I hope this won't take long, Marshall." She gave him her best polite smile, trying to hide the way her insides were wiggling like jelly. "I don't want to be late for the meeting. You shouldn't be either."

Marshall inhaled slowly through both nostrils, and then he exhaled. "Julia, you're not going to be at the meeting. There's no need for your services in this new advertising deal."

She felt as though the floor was tilting slightly, she was so stunned. "What—what do you mean?" She shook her head, not sure what to make of his statement. "What on earth are you talking about?"

Marshall inhaled slowly and then exhaled again. "I mean, that as a matter of fact—" He paused, taking another inhale and exhale. It was clear to her that he was searching for his words. "We've decided to do away with your position altogether."

Her jaw dropped, and her body felt hot and then cold all over.

"You're firing me?"

Marshall cleared his throat delicately, still avoiding eye contact.

"On a Monday morning? Ten—no, seven minutes before a major meeting with a potential client? You realize I studied for this meeting, Marshall? I did work on this." Her shock was quickly giving way to anger. "Am I really being fired?"

"I wasn't choosing that terminology, but—"

"You couldn't find one moment this weekend to tell me? You couldn't even send an email or a text? I had to get all dressed up and come down here so I could pack up my desk while everyone's here to see me walk out?"

Although his expression remained blank, the tips of Marshall's ears were starting to turn slightly pink. "I've been busy preparing for this meeting."

"What kind of a lame excuse is that? I've been busy all weekend preparing too. And for what? I did all that work for nothing."

He cleared his throat. "I concede that I should have found the time to let you know sooner."

She stared at him, still reeling from the news. Her anger was beginning to shift into an unpleasant feeling that was similar to getting punched in the stomach. For a few moments, she struggled to get any words out, and then she stammered, "Why am I being fired?"

He glanced at his watch, frowning and twitching his shoulders a little.

"It's nothing personal, Julia, just the usual downsizing that all companies have to do from time to time. Unfortunately, I don't have a lot of time to discuss this right now. I have the meeting with Cutie Pie, and I don't want to be late." He hesitated for a moment, and then said, "I'll send you the details via email, along with information about your severance package. And the final documentation of your termination, of course."

A million thoughts seemed to race through her brain at once.

She wondered why Marshall thought that it was unpleasant to say the word "fired," but he seemed to have no problem using the word "termination." She wondered why he couldn't have just taken a few minutes to fire her over email if that was how he was choosing to really explain the whole thing to her anyway. She wondered what on earth she was going to do, where was she going to go next.

Marshall cleared his throat gently and Julia stood, feeling stunned. She didn't say goodbye to him, she simply walked out the door and down the hallway to her office. Her one consolation, she thought bitterly, was that most people would be in the meeting while she was leaving Caldunski Inc. with her stuff and she wouldn't have an audience for her departure.

She had to blink back tears as she took down her pictures, utensil holders, and knickknacks and began to stuff them all into her purse. It was a large purse, and they almost all fit, but not quite. She had to sneak past the meeting room to get an empty cardboard box from the mail room. She could hear the sounds of the meeting going on, and she winced, wishing she could be in there to share all of her ideas.

As she was leaving the building, a wave of nostalgia swept over her. She'd been so excited for that job, so sure that it was her next step in climbing the ladder of success. Now there she was, being ushered out with her tail between her legs.

She took a back door out onto the sidewalk, since she didn't want to walk through the lobby and be seen by everyone who was getting into the elevators. She wasn't dressed for showing up to the office to clean out her desk—she was dressed for a meeting. It looked like she'd done something terrible within the first five minutes of work and gotten thrown out on her ear.

She strode across the sidewalk, feeling dazed as she tried to hail a cab. Her head was spinning, and she knew she needed to try to concoct some kind of plan, but she was still reeling from the shock and disappointment and hurt of it all.

What on earth had just happened?

CHAPTER TWO

Julia took a sip of her salted caramel crew cold brew coffee, trying to find a sense of peace in the middle of the busy coffee shop. She took a deep breath, looking out at the bustling New York sidewalk through the window beside her, and then closed her eyes for a moment.

It was Wednesday, two days after she'd been fired. She'd been completely useless the day before, allowing herself to eat only slices of pizza and watch movies all day while wearing fleece sweatpants and a baggy t-shirt. After her one day of vegging out, however, she was feeling restless and ready for action again. She'd already started putting out feelings for new jobs, although nothing looked promising—or interesting—to her.

She'd come there to her favorite upscale New York coffee shop to meet with her best friend, Dana, who would be arriving at any moment. She took another sip of her coffee and sighed. It tasted delicious, and the extra shot of espresso seemed to be already working its magic, but she scolded herself for spending six dollars on a coffee when she didn't have a job.

I'm used to having enough money for everything, she thought, feeling her stomach flop. *Enough money for food, clothes, makeup, and fancy drinks like this. I've got to get used to not having any extra money, at least for a while.*

She bit her lip. She had a decent amount of savings, but life in New York was insanely expensive, and she couldn't afford to be without a job for long.

She glanced at her watch, wondering where Dana was. Curiously, she turned her head toward the doors to the coffee shop, and then a smile spread across her face as she saw her friend stepping inside. She lifted a hand in greeting and Dana hurried over to her table.

"Girl, what's up?" Dana gave Julia a hug, looking worried. Dana always wore bright colors and smelled faintly of citrus. Julia smiled weakly and sat back down.

"You should go get your drink. I'll be right here." She'd told herself that the words would come easily as soon as she saw her best friend, but now she realized that she needed some time to gather her thoughts. She wanted to tell Dana all about getting fired, and at the same time, she didn't want to talk about it at all.

"Okay. I got a mobile order, so I'll be back in a flash."

Dana returned in less than a minute, holding a large iced coffee. She sat down across from Julia, looking worried. "You look worn out."

Julia shrugged and tried to laugh off her friend's words. "I mean, I've gotten a lot more sleep than usual the past two nights. In theory. I've gotten to sleep in, but I keep waking up and tossing and turning. So I shouldn't have any massively dark circles under my eyes or anything."

Dana shook her head, looking confused. "What on earth are you saying? What happened?"

"I'm just saying that I probably look worn out because I'm not all dolled-up like usual. Because why? Because I have no one to impress."

Dana leaned forward, giving her friend a kind but slightly reprimanding look. "Julia. What happened?"

Julia bit her lip, trying to fight back the tears that had sprung into her eyes. "I got fired."

"No." Dana reached across the table and squeezed Julia's hand. "I don't believe it. Why?"

"Oh, well apparently they're eliminating my position altogether." She let out a bitter laugh. "But it's more than that. My boss didn't even explain it all to me in person, but he sent an email after I'd left with all my stuff."

"How warm," Dana said sarcastically, looking indignant.

Julia nodded. "He said that even though my work has been great—I mean, my events have all been so successful in the past year, and he acknowledged that—one of my coworkers, Cheryl, kept reporting me as difficult to work with. I mean, I guess I was kind of difficult to work with at times, but not to the extent that I should be fired! I was just trying to do my job as efficiently as possible. And besides, I essentially got fired because of a lie. What really did it was that Cheryl accused me of sabotaging other members of the team in favor of gaining recognition for myself." She felt the tears rush into her eyes again, with more intensity this time. She blinked them back and took a deep breath, shaking her head. "I would never do that. I know

Cheryl didn't like me, but I can't believe she would do something like this. And I trusted Marshall—I thought he had my back. But he didn't even stand up for me and or let me tell him my side of the story." A couple of the tears slipped out and she wiped them hurriedly away.

"Well, first of all, you show me what this Cheryl looks like and if I ever see her on the street I'm going to 'accidentally' spill coffee all over her." Dana's eyes widened with indignation, and she brandished her coffee cup emphatically.

Julia laughed, feeling encouraged by her friend's support. "No, don't do that. It's in the past now. If that's what my workplace was really like behind my back, then I don't want to be there anymore. I just have to figure out what I'm going to do next."

"Something better will open up, I'm sure of it. You're going to find a better job, with better coworkers, and maybe even make more money. This isn't the end of the world."

Julia tried to smile bravely at her friend's optimism. She was grateful for Dana's words, but she couldn't quite believe them. She knew it wasn't really the end of the world, but it still felt that way.

At that moment, Dana's phone buzzed on the

table, and she looked down at the text message that had just come in.

"Oh, no." Dana ran her fingers through her hair, looking suddenly frazzled. "Julia, I've got to go, I'm so sorry. There's a work emergency and they need me there ASAP."

Julia's heart twisted in disappointment, but she smiled as if it was no big deal. "No worries. Thanks for being here for a little while, at least."

Both friends stood up and hugged.

"I'm buying you magazines and ice cream and a really soft blanket," Dana said as they pulled away from the hug.

"Don't do that." Julia laughed. "I had my couch potato day yesterday. I don't want to just lie around anymore. I need to figure out what I'm going to do next."

"Okay, fine, just the ice cream." Dana winked, and then her phone buzzed again. "Ahh, this is such an inconvenience. I've really got to go. I'll call you later. Love you!"

"Love you!"

Julia waved and smiled as Dana hurried out of the front door of the coffee shop. Then she sat down in her chair, suddenly feeling overwhelmingly tired.

Dana getting called back to work might be an

inconvenience, but at least she has a job to get called back to, she thought, feeling her stomach slosh with worry. *She's lucky.*

She took another sip of her coffee, wondering what she was going to do with the rest of her day. She should apply to more jobs, that was for sure, but she—

Her phone began to ring, and she pulled it out of her purse, thinking it was probably Dana. Her eyebrows lifted in surprise when she saw that the caller was her sister, Hazel.

She hadn't talked to her sister in a while, and her first thought was that Hazel had somehow found out about her getting fired and was calling to offer condolences. Then she realized that would be impossible, since there would have been no way for Hazel to hear about it unless Julia had told her herself. Hazel still lived in their sleepy little hometown of Rosewood Beach in Connecticut, far away from the bustle and gossip of New York.

She didn't feel ready to tell Hazel her bad news yet—she didn't feel like talking about it, and she didn't want to start crying in the middle of the coffee shop again. Still, she told herself that she would have to tell her eventually, so it might as well be now. She steeled herself for the possibility of unveiling her bad news.

"Hey, Hazel." She tried to make her voice sound cheerful as she answered the phone. "What's up?"

"Hey, Julia."

As soon as she heard her sister's voice, Julia knew that something was wrong. Hazel's voice sounded tired—heavy even—and a little stuffy, as if she'd been crying.

"Hey." Julia didn't know what else to say. It was like all other words had flown out of her mind. A cloudy premonition fell over her, and she felt her stomach sink like a rock. She waited, her heart hammering, for Hazel to say more.

"I'm calling because I have bad news." There was a pause while Hazel took a deep breath. Julia held her phone tighter, staring at the center of the coffee table in front of her. "Dad passed away."

CHAPTER THREE

Cooper Harris rubbed his eyes, trying to stifle a yawn as he sat at his desk. It was another quiet workday at his job at Greener Pastures Landscaping Company, and he was trying to stay focused despite how sleepy he was.

He glanced out the window, looking at the way the early morning sunlight was adding a golden hue to the charming streets of Rosewood Beach. He smiled quietly to himself and leaned back to stretch.

I've got to figure out some way to get Macey to sleep better at night, he thought. *I can't keep staying up half the night with her like this. I'm still groggy even after I've had my coffee.*

Macey, his adorable two-year-old daughter, had been having trouble sleeping lately, and he wasn't sure what to do about it. Whenever she woke up and called for him, he would go into her room and read to her for a while or get her some water or milk to drink. Sometimes those things worked, but more often than not, they didn't. He guessed that his little girl was missing her mother, and that was making her restless and fitful.

He swallowed, feeling a wave of missing his late wife wash over him. He never thought he'd have to be doing life without her—raising their baby without her—but there he was, and it was harder than he ever would have imagined.

He shook himself, refusing to get down in the dumps about his situation. It was hard, certainly, but he was making the best of it and would continue to do so. He was going to build an amazing life there in Rosewood Beach for Macey and himself.

He'd first heard about the town when he was doing research on places to move to. After his wife had passed away, he'd decided to sell his ranch in Colorado and use the money to give himself and his daughter a fresh start somewhere quieter. He'd felt that it would be easier to raise his daughter as a single dad in a town like Rosewood Beach than it would be to raise her out in the mountain country, far away from the surrounding towns, while still doing the taxing work of running a busy ranch. When he'd seen the pictures of Rosewood Beach in a magazine, he'd been struck by how picturesque it looked. He'd never lived right next to the water before, but he'd always liked the idea of being close to the ocean. Once he'd secured a job in the town, he and Macey had made the move from Colorado to Connecticut, and they were now settled in a cozy new home.

He didn't regret his decision—Rosewood Beach was a great town, and he was enjoying living there— but he'd expected the move to make his life at least somewhat easy, and that hadn't been the case at all.

He sighed, looking out the window again. There was nothing easy about being without his wife.

He closed his eyes, fighting back another wave of grief. It still came and went, and it was feeling acutely painful less often, but sometimes it still felt like his chest was filled with ice. His wife had died unexpectedly in a car accident, and he'd found himself having to be both father and mother to his little girl. Although he tried to be everything for Macey, he often felt stretched thin, and as though no matter what he did, he couldn't make up for the fact that she didn't have a mother in her life anymore.

He sighed again and picked up his coffee mug,

bringing it to his lips. He discovered that it was empty and put it down in disappointment.

At that moment, his boss, Austin, stepped into the room. "Morning, Harris." Austin smiled at him good-naturedly, looking slightly amused. "You look like you could use a jumpstart."

Cooper chuckled. "I am feeling pretty groggy this morning. My little one kept me up half the night."

"Ooh, they'll do that." Austin's smile was sympathetic. He knew that Cooper was a single father. "You should take a break and head over to Ocean Breeze Café. Get some coffee and maybe something to eat. You look like you need it."

"That's a good idea. You sure you're okay with me stepping away for a while?"

"Sure. I mean, don't take all day—but in case you haven't noticed, business is slow right now." He shrugged genially.

Smiling, Cooper stood up. "Well, thanks, Austin. I'll be back soon."

Ocean Breeze Café was only a short walk from the Greener Pastures offices. Cooper stuffed his hands into the pockets of his light jacket and began to whistle as he strolled down the sidewalk. It was a beautiful day outside, with wispy white clouds sailing across a backdrop of bright blue. He wondered how Macey was doing at her daycare—he hadn't gotten any calls or messages about her crying a lot, so that was a good sign. She wasn't prone to crying, really, just that kind of restless energy that had been keeping both of them up at night.

He soon reached Ocean Breeze Café and stepped inside. He'd been to the cozy, popular coffee shop a few times before, since the place had been recommended to him the very first day he'd arrived in Rosewood Beach. He breathed in the woodsy aroma of the coffee, feeling eager to order a cup.

"Hey there, cowboy." Sally Lipton, the middle-aged owner of Ocean Breeze Café, grinned at him warmly from behind the counter. "How's your day going?"

"Hi, Sally."

He smiled at her. She was one of the nicest people in town, and always remembered her customers. She might have been a "spinster," but she put the best spin on her situation that he'd ever seen in anyone. She wore bright colors, crazy hair pieces, and always sported a cheerful bubble gum pink lipstick. She looked fun and she was fun, and she was always eager to make everyone's day better. He liked her a lot—not only because of her kind, cheerful attitude, but also because she was the first person who had been able to coax a smile out of Macey when they'd first moved to town.

"How's business?" he asked.

"Great as usual." Her eyes were bright, and she straightened the glittery purple butterfly clip that she had tucked into her hair. "What can I get for you?"

"Just a regular coffee with a little cream. I'm a plain fellow." He grinned, and she laughed.

"Lots of people like their coffee that same way. I like to make the fancy drinks, but my coffee is good enough to stand on its own two feet."

She hummed cheerfully as she made him his coffee. He looked around the pleasant shop while he waited, telling himself he'd have to bring Macey there again sometime soon. She'd liked it there a lot, and she'd liked Sally.

"You look tired, if you don't mind me saying so, Cooper." Sally's eyes looked sympathetic as she handed him his coffee cup.

He nodded. "I am. I was up half the night with Macey. She's been restless a lot lately."

"You poor thing. Tell you what: if you're willing to stick around for another few minutes, I'll throw in a corned beef sandwich on the house."

"Thanks, Sally. That's really sweet of you." He

smiled at her, and his stomach grumbled as if in agreement.

"No problem at all. You need a little extra fuel today, that's clear."

He paid for the coffee, and then sipped it slowly while waiting for Sally to make the sandwich. He felt himself perk up a little, and he rolled his shoulders back a few times, trying to wake himself up even more.

"There you are," Sally said a few minutes later, handing him a white paper bag. "I make the best corned beef sandwich in town."

"I believe it." He grinned at her. "Thank you again."

"Come back soon!"

"Oh, I will, don't worry."

He waved goodbye and made his way back outside. The moment he did, he frowned and took a few steps back, discovering that it was raining hard.

Well, that snuck up on me, he thought, glancing up at the sky in surprise. *It's really rare for it to rain like this during this time of year.*

He pulled up the collar of his work shirt—which was already dirty with half-dried paint from a job he'd been on earlier that morning—and started back toward the office. He didn't mind rain so much, since he loved the way it smelled, although he had to reconcile himself to the fact that he would be soaked by the time he got back to his desk. At least his work shirt was thick, and he could take it off once he got back inside.

He saw that the ground along the sidewalk was already getting muddy. In some places, puddles were collecting along the gaps between the grass and the sidewalk.

Just in front of him along the road, a taxi pulled up to the curb, catching his attention. He didn't often see taxis in this small town, except for when travelers hired a cab to drive them to Rosewood Beach from the nearest airport.

He kept walking, assuming that whoever was inside the taxi was going to take a minute or two to get out, since it was raining particularly hard at the moment.

Instead of waiting, however, the person inside the taxi opened the door abruptly, almost hitting him as he walked past. He jumped to the side, surprised, as a woman whom he'd never seen before stepped out of the taxi.

"Ugh!" The woman hunched her shoulders up against the rain, looking irritated. Instead of getting back inside the taxi, she stepped forward, stumbling a little on her fancy looking heels. She missed the edge of the sidewalk—probably because it was difficult to see because of how hard it was raining—and placed one heel squarely in a patch of squelching mud. She let out a squeak and started to wobble, veering toward the muddy ground to her left.

Cooper realized she was about to fall, and he threw his coffee and sandwich bag down onto the sidewalk. He darted forward, catching the woman just before she completely lost her balance.

For a moment, she froze, looking stunned, and he thought to himself that she was extremely beautiful. She had long dark hair and sharply attractive features, which she'd accented with expertly-done makeup.

He helped her back up to her feet, and she started to frown, looking at his work shirt. As he removed his arms from her, she lifted up the sleeve of her black raincoat and winced clear in dismay.

"You got paint on me." She held up the sleeve of her coat, revealing a smear of white paint.

"Sorry." He grinned at her. "My work shirt is still drying. Better some paint than a face full of mud, though, right?"

She scowled down at her muddy shoes. A few

moments passed, and he could feel water dripping down the back of his head. "Well, thank you," she said stiffly.

She turned away from him, back to the taxi, where she started to get a suitcase out of the trunk.

Realizing the interaction was over, he stooped down and picked up his now-empty coffee cup and the soggy sandwich bag. At least the sandwich itself was inside a waterproof Styrofoam to-go box.

He shook his head as he went on his way. He was soaked to the bone, and he let out a sigh, glancing back at the woman for a moment. It seemed coffee and a favorable interaction with a beautiful woman weren't in the cards for him today. At least he still had his corned beef sandwich.

CHAPTER FOUR

Julia stood on the sidewalk in the rain, holding the handle of her rolling suitcase tightly. She stared at the familiar restaurant in front of her, The Lighthouse Grill, Rosewood Beach's most beloved local pub.

A wave of nostalgia swept over her, and also a sudden reluctance to go inside. It was her family's restaurant, and she'd grown up surrounded by its friendly customers, cheerful noise, and mouthwatering smells. Now, however, things were different. Her father had passed away, and she was a whole new person. She didn't know how it would feel to go back inside, and even though it was raining, a few seconds passed before she could bring herself to start walking toward the door.

She stopped under the striped awning, where raindrops were still dripping down occasionally but it was generally out of the downpour. She inspected her raincoat and her muddy heel, wanting to make herself look more presentable before going inside. She took a tissue out of her tissue pocket pack and wiped some of the mud off her shoe. Then she turned to her coat sleeve, frowning in frustration as she looked at the paint that was flaking across it.

She brushed her hand over it, and to her relief, most of the paint came off in flakes. Only a few small spots remained, and she knew she would be able to get those out with a little laundry magic.

She thought about the handsome stranger who had caught her so unexpectedly. He'd had very kind eyes, and she'd realized as he was leaving that he'd dropped his coffee to catch her.

I shouldn't have been so rude to him, she thought regretfully, picking at one of the remaining pieces of dried paint on her coat sleeve.

She'd let the stress she was still feeling over losing her job and joining her family for her father's funeral get the better of her. The mud all over her shoes had felt like the final straw, but then it had turned out that seeing white paint smeared across the sleeve of her favorite coat had been the final straw. She'd snapped a little with frustration because it had all felt like too much at once.

She glanced down the sidewalk in the direction he'd kept walking in. He was out of sight by that time, but she found herself wondering where he'd gone. She almost had an impulse to run after him and apologize for how rude she'd been. She was still frustrated that he'd gotten paint on her coat, but he'd meant to be kind.

And more than that, she felt drawn to him in a way she couldn't quite explain.

He might have been dirty, rugged, and rough around the edges, but there was something oddly magnetic about him. She'd looked at him long enough to appreciate the slight wave in his almost-black hair and the brightness in his chestnut-colored eyes.

She found herself secretly hoping that she would get a chance to see him again. She looked down the sidewalk in the direction he'd gone again, trying to speculate about where he might have been coming from.

Don't be silly, Julia, she told herself. *It's been so long since you were in town, everything's probably completely different from how it used to be.*

Turning back to The Lighthouse Grill, she took a

deep breath. There was no point in procrastinating the moment any longer. She needed to go in there and talk to her family members.

She reached out and touched the door handle. It seemed to mold to her touch, and with the familiar feeling of it came back a host of memories that had been half-buried in her mind. She took a deep breath, smelling the familiar savory aromas of the restaurant, and it was as if part of her was being transported into the past.

Her throat tightened a little as emotions swept through her. Her parents had run that place for as long as she had been alive, and she had just as many memories of The Lighthouse Grill as she did of her childhood home.

She took another deep breath, tugged on the door handle, and stepped inside.

It did feel a little bit as though she was going back in time. The room was filled with memories, darting through her mind like ghosts. She couldn't help smiling, but at the same time, an achy feeling filled her chest.

Nostalgia washed over her as she rolled her suitcase through the dining room. Her eyes traced over the familiar booths and tables, and the sound of people laughing and clinking their silverware reminded her of all the times she'd heard those sounds there before. The scent of fried fish and tater tots permeated the air, and she took a deep breath, feeling her stomach grumble. She was unable to keep from smiling over how good it smelled. Her family's restaurant was the most popular pub in Rosewood Beach for a reason.

She made her way to the swinging wooden doors that led into the kitchen. She pushed them open carefully, knowing how busy the kitchen always was, and as soon as she poked her head inside, she heard people call out her name in excitement.

The next thing she knew she was being crushed in a hug by Allison, who had been working at The Lighthouse Grill since it opened, and patted on the back by Tom, another one of the cooks who had known her since she was a little girl.

"Look at you." Allison was grinning from ear to ear, and she adjusted the hair net that covered her silver hair. "So tall and elegant."

"Well, the tall part is because of these." Julia laughed and lifted her foot to point out how tall her heels were.

Tom whistled. "Don't you trip in those things?"

"Uh, sometimes." She grimaced. "But enough

about me—how are you two doing? How's this old place been holding up?"

"Oh, we're great." Tom leaned against the wall, grinning. "Still kicking and screaming. And this place is as popular as ever."

"Mm, more so." Allison nodded, looking proud. "We're all getting even better at our jobs, and the reputation of the place is so engrained in the town by now that almost everyone who passes through stops here for dinner."

"Or lunch. Or breakfast." Tom lifted his brows.

Julia laughed, realizing how much she'd missed the two of them and their cheerful senses of humor. The sadness of her father's passing hovered over their conversation, and all of them seemed alert to each other's feelings, but no one said anything about it out loud for a few moments. Finally, after a long pause, Allison reached out again and hugged Julia around the shoulders with one arm.

"Glad you're back, kiddo. I'm sorry for the reason why."

Julia felt a lump rise up in her throat, and she had to blink back a few tears. "Me too." She nodded, and there was silence between the three of them for a few moments. Tom swallowed, looking at the floor.

"You want to see your mom?" Allison smiled, bringing sunshine back into their conversation.

"Yeah, I do." Julia took a deep breath, returning Allison's smile. "Is she in her office?"

"That she is." Allison gestured to another door at the back of the kitchen, which Julia knew led down a short hallway to her mother's office at the back of the building. "I'm sure she can't wait to see you. We should let you keep moving."

Julia nodded, smiling at them. "I'll see you both soon. I—I'll be here for a while." Her stomach twisted.

At that moment, one of the pans of cooking food made a loud sizzling sound. "And we've got to get back to work!" Tom laughed. "We're going to burn this place down if we're not careful."

Julia smiled at them both one more time, and then made her way through the doorway that led toward her mother's office. The achy feeling in her chest returned as she walked along the wooden floorboards to the white-painted door that had a flower-themed calendar hanging on it.

She knocked softly on it, swallowing. A second later, her mother's voice called out, "Come on in."

Julia pushed open the door and saw the familiar

desk, covered in papers, and her mother, seated in front of an open laptop.

Vivian Owens looked up and gasped when she saw her daughter. Julia felt tears spring into her eyes as she saw her mother leap up and hurry toward her for a hug. They embraced, holding each other tightly, and as Julia took a deep breath, she realized that her mother had always smelled faintly of honey and lavender. She breathed in the smell, feeling the sense of comfort that only her mother could give to her.

"My girl." Vivian rocked her back and forth a few times. "I'm so happy to see you."

Over her mother's shoulder, Julia could see the internet page that Vivian had been looking at, and it was clearly the website of a funeral parlor. Her heart sank, realizing that her mother was right in the middle of funeral arrangements.

"Can I do anything for you?" Julia asked a little breathlessly as they pulled out of the hug. She was trying not to cry, and she offered her mother a brave smile. "Anything at all?"

"For now, just stand there and let me look at you." Vivian held her daughter's shoulders, beaming at her. "You look so elegant. So grown up."

"I'm thirty-four, Mom. Of course I look grown up."

Julia had to blink back tears again, since the way her mother was treating her like her little girl was bringing back all kinds of sweet memories of her childhood.

Vivian touched her daughter's cheek and whispered, "Your father was so proud of you."

Julia couldn't stop the tears from coming then, and she wiped them off her cheeks. "I'm sorry for not being around much recently, Mom. I wish I had been. I'm sorry."

Vivian shook her head. "You couldn't possibly have known what would happen. None of us did. It's so sad." She took a trembling breath, and Julia squeezed her hand.

"It is. We all thought we had so many more years with him."

For a moment, the two of them stood there holding tightly to each other's hands without speaking.

"But I am sorry, Mom." Julia's voice was soft. "I wish I'd been here."

"Don't you worry." Vivian shook her head, giving her daughter a brave smile. "I know you put a lot of effort into your job, and that's why you're so successful, working at that big company in New York. I bet it's no time at all until you get a promotion."

Her mother's praise felt like a stab to Julia's heart. She swallowed, wondering if she should come right out and tell her mother what had happened. She hesitated for a brief moment, torn between wanting to be honest and not wanting to feel even worse in that moment than she already did, and then she decided that she would tell her mother soon, but not quite yet.

"How's everyone else doing?" Julia asked, wanting to change the subject. She took a seat in the chair placed opposite her mother's desk.

Vivian sighed, sitting down again in her own chair. "Oh, how can anyone really be doing at a time like this? But everyone's been hanging in there. Dean and Hazel have been helping me with the funeral arrangements ever since—well, ever since it happened—and Alexis arrived from Los Angeles yesterday."

Julia nodded, suddenly missing her siblings very much and looking forward to seeing them. Dean and Hazel lived there in Rosewood Beach. Dean was a mechanic who was sweet and affable, and suited to small-town life. Hazel had got married straight out of high school, and although she had gotten divorced soon after, she'd had a beautiful baby girl who was now twelve years old. Alexis was the only one of the siblings besides Julia who had left Rosewood Beach. After she'd graduated high school, Alexis had pursued a career in modeling and had been fairly successful. She only modeled on and off now, since her husband Grayson made a great deal of money and could easily support them without a paycheck from his wife. Julia realized with a pang of regret that it had been a while since she'd really caught up with any of her siblings, and she didn't know much about the current details of their lives.

"Having you all here is going to be such a comfort to me." Vivian smiled, taking a deep breath. "It's definitely going to help with the transition into living life without Frank." For a moment, she didn't say anything more. She stared into space, looking sad and dazed. "Well," she said finally, forcing another smile. "At least I still have security in the business, huh?"

Julia reached out and squeezed her mother's hand. "Yes, you do. This place will be standing for another hundred years."

The two of them shared a smile, and Julia took a deep breath. She wondered how it was going to be, diving back into being around the siblings she hadn't seen in so long.

CHAPTER FIVE

Alexis Bennett opened her eyes and stared at the ceiling above her. She was still a little groggy from sleep, and at first, she felt confused, wondering why she wasn't in her room at home. Her own bedroom that she shared with her husband Grayson—well, which she shared with her husband when he wasn't out of town on business trips or sleeping in the den downstairs because of getting home from the office in the middle of the night—had a crystal beaded chandelier and ornate ceiling tiles. This ceiling was plain and white and had a faint water stain in one corner.

In the next instant, she remembered everything. She remembered that she'd returned to Rosewood Beach because of the tragedy, and she shut her eyes tightly, trying to ward off the grief of losing her father. She lay perfectly still in bed, listening to the sound of raindrops pattering against the windowpane, and the faint whooshing sound of a car passing on the street outside.

She was back. Back in Rosewood Beach, in her childhood hometown. Perhaps it would have felt even more strange to be back in her childhood room, but she wasn't staying in her old home with her mother. She hadn't wanted to give Vivian one more thing to deal with, and since she hadn't spent any time with her sister Hazel or Hazel's twelve-year-old daughter Samantha for a long while, she'd decided to stay in their house with them.

She opened her eyes again, looking at the ceiling. She stared at the water stain for a few moments, and then let out a sigh. Hazel's house was cute—small, charming, whimsical, and decorated in a cottage-like style. Hazel and Samantha had clearly put a lot of effort into making their home a place they both loved, and it was a pleasant place to be in even for someone like Alexis, who was used to a very high-end style of living. But Hazel's house was old and falling apart in places. A few of the doors needed new hinges—or they needed to be replaced entirely—and then there were things like that water stain.

Alexis hadn't seen any of her siblings very often because she lived so far away, in L.A. She was glad she had the time to bond with Samantha and catch up with Hazel, but she wished she'd known they needed some extra money the way they clearly did. She'd known that things must have been difficult for Hazel, raising a daughter all on her own, but she wished she'd thought to ask her if she needed help or money. She could easily spare the money it would take to fix up Hazel's house.

No, she wouldn't accept It anyway, Alexis thought, smiling a little to herself. *She's always been so independent. The wild child.*

Although Hazel wasn't so wild anymore, now that she had a daughter to raise. She clearly took her role as a parent seriously, and Alexis was proud of how well Hazel was taking care of Samantha. She'd worked hard to build a good life for the two of them, and Alexis almost felt jealous that Hazel had gotten to put so much effort into her personal life. She herself was beginning to feel like a hamster, running around in circles in a gilded cage.

She rolled over onto her side and closed her eyes again. She missed modeling work, although she still got to do it now and again, but that wasn't what had been making her feel so uncomfortable in her personal life. On the surface, her life was picture perfect. She had an incredible house and a handsome husband whose job allowed them to be very well off. In theory, she could relax and let herself enjoy her comfortable life, spending time with friends and experiencing luxurious living in L.A. But she wasn't comfortable being idle, especially since Grayson had become more and more preoccupied with work. She could feel him drifting away from their relationship, and without work of her own to focus on, the problems in her marriage weighed more heavily on her mind than they should. She'd taken up jewelry design as a hobby, and she enjoyed it very much, but a hobby didn't use up enough of her restless energy the way a job would have.

The truth was, she didn't know what to do. She'd tried to put a spark back Into her marriage, but Grayson had remained distant. She'd already been feeling lost and troubled, unsure of how to tell anyone that her reality was so different from how her life looked on paper, when the news of her father's death had arrived.

She took a deep breath, blinking back the tears that were filling her eyes. Her already emotionally fragile state, combined with her grief about her

father, had made returning to Rosewood Beach
difficult for her. It had been a long time since she'd
visited, and she was having a hard time being in a
place that felt both very strange and very familiar at
the same time. She got the impression that people in
her hometown found her a little too aloof, or even
stuck-up, but she was used to talking and acting the
way people in L.A. did, and the small-town ways of
Rosewood Beach seemed strangely laid-back to
her now.

At least Julia is here, she thought, smiling a little
to herself as she thought about her other sister's
arrival.

Even though she hadn't seen Julia for quite some
time, she was glad she wasn't the only city girl in the
family. It made her feel less like some kind of black
sheep. She and Julia both led lives that were a far cry
from the ways of Rosewood Beach, and she felt sure
that would make it easy for the two of them to get on
common ground and support each other during the
days ahead.

Feeling somewhat better, she sat up, wiping the
last stray tears off her cheeks. She slid out of bed and
went into the bathroom to wash her face and apply a
variety of face creams. Once she'd gotten dressed

into chic and expensive athleticwear, she stepped out of her room, feeling strangely shy.

She smelled something wonderful coming from the kitchen downstairs, and she inhaled, noting that she definitely smelled bacon and some kind of baked good. Smiling, she made her way down the staircase and to the kitchen, where Samantha and Hazel were bustling around, laughing together about something.

Alexis smiled. It felt good to see her family members smile in the middle of what they were all going through. And it was clear that Hazel and Samantha had a good life, helping each other out and enjoying a cheerful home life together. That warmed her heart, and she felt another surge of pride for her sister.

"Good morning," she said, stepping into the cozy kitchen, which was filled with the sound of sizzling food and the clink of dishes.

"Good morning!" Samantha said, immediately throwing her arms around her aunt and giving her a hug. "I was thinking last night, and I have a question for you—I was wondering if you would help me pick out an outfit for a party that we're having at school? It's not like a big dance or anything, so I don't have to wear a dress, although I could wear a dress. It would just be a kind of nice dress, instead of a really nice dress. Mom's good about clothes and stuff but I know you must really know a lot about fashion because you live in L.A. And I was wondering if you would help me decorate my room a little bit? I have all these posters but I'm having trouble deciding where to put them."

"Easy, tiger." Hazel laughed, turning around from where she was cooking bacon at the stove. "There will be plenty of time for all that. Let your aunt get settled in."

"Okay." Samantha smiled, looking as though she might be holding back some wiggles of enthusiasm.

"What's on the menu?" Alexis asked, smiling. "It smells incredible in here."

"Oh, just wait," Samantha said, her brown eyes shining. Her long blonde hair was pulled back in a French braid, which was so messy it looked as though she'd slept in it. She had a streak of flour on her cheek, but she looked as proud as the owner of a gourmet restaurant. Hazel had told Alexis that Samantha was very excited that both of her aunts were back in town, and Alexis had the feeling she was eager to make a good impression. "We have bacon, as you can see, frittatas, apple turnovers, and orange juice. Freshly squeezed orange juice, I might add."

"Wow." Alexis smiled, genuinely impressed. "Good job. Do you guys normally make this much food for breakfast?"

"We do." Hazel grinned, looking proud of that. "Although we're not usually quite this gourmet—the apple turnovers and the frittatas at once was an endeavor."

"Which we succeeded in." Samantha nodded her head triumphantly.

Alexis laughed. "Can I help with anything?"

"No, we should be good, but thanks for asking. The table's all set, and this bacon should be done in another minute or so. Oh, I guess you could take the apple turnovers off the cooling rack and put them in that bowl."

A few minutes later, they were sitting down to eat the delicious meal together. Alexis's stomach grumbled, and she smiled in satisfaction as she brought her glass of fresh-squeezed orange juice to her lips.

"Thank you so much for letting me stay here," she said, reaching out and hugging Hazel around the shoulders. "You're being so hospitable. You'll have to let me return the favor somehow."

"Well, you can help Samantha out with all her projects if you want." Hazel smiled as the hug broke and they went back to their meals. "She is very excited about your L.A. expertise. And I think it would be fun for the two of you to bond."

"I agree." Alexis smiled at Samantha, who grinned back at her.

For a few minutes, they ate their breakfast in silence. All of the food was delicious, and Alexis remarked that she'd never had apple turnovers that good. Hazel laughed as though she hadn't meant it sincerely, but she had. The frittatas were filled with mushrooms, spinach, and tomatoes, and they practically melted in her mouth. She felt new energy fill her as she ate the nourishing food.

"So what about you, Alexis?" Hazel's blue-green eyes lit with interest, and she brushed back a strand of her long, wavy dark blonde hair. She smiled, revealing the dimples in her cheeks. "How's your life back in the fabulous city of Los Angeles?"

"Oh, things are all right." Alexis forced a smile. She was determined to be honest with her sister, but she also didn't feel much like talking about all of the things that had been weighing on her mind lately.

A few seconds of silence elapsed, and then Hazel pressed her sister for more information. "What do you mean 'all right'? Is something wrong? I thought you and Grayson were out there living the dream.

All of your pictures make your house seem like some kind of castle, and make you seem like some kind of princess."

Alexis laughed, feeling an ache at her sister's words. "Well, thank you. But there aren't any red-headed princesses."

"Oh, yes there are!" Samantha protested. "And Mom's right, you look really beautiful in all those pictures."

Alexis's heart warmed. It was a long time since she'd felt beautiful, and their words were a pleasant reminder that she was still attractive. Her long reddish-brown hair was complemented by a few freckles on her nose and her vibrant green eyes. Her figure was tall and willowy, and her features were beautiful enough while still being unique enough to have gotten her some great modeling jobs during the height of her career.

"Well, thank you both. That's sweet of you to say." She smiled, hoping the conversation would drift naturally to other things.

Hazel seemed to be determined to know more about Alexis's life, however. "Is something the matter? You looked really down when you said that things were just 'all right.'"

Alexis sighed, shaking her head. "Things—well, I think everything feels weighty now, because of Dad."

Hazel nodded, blinking back some tears. "I understand what you mean. Grief isn't like what I expected. I thought I'd be crying all the time. But it's more like there's this constant ache underneath everything, and then sometimes the pain gets really sharp."

Alexis nodded, knowing just what her sister meant. She'd still had moments of happiness even after hearing about their father's death, but underneath it all had been the deep sadness of knowing that he was gone.

"But I do want to hear more about your life," Hazel insisted, forcing a brave smile. "What are you up to these days?"

"Oh, not much." Alexis sighed, looking out the window and noticing how lovely Hazel and Samantha's garden looked in the sunlight. "I don't do as much modeling work anymore, since I've mostly aged out of it. That makes me feel as though I've lost some of my identity. I want something to do with myself, but there's nothing to do, really. Grayson works very long hours—sometimes I don't see him at all, because he comes home late, goes to sleep downstairs, and then leaves in the morning before I wake up."

Hazel nodded, looking sympathetic and troubled. Alexis's stomach flopped as she wondered what Hazel was thinking about her marriage. It didn't sound very romantic, that was for sure.

"It's been hard." Alexis took another sip of the orange juice, feeling a little cheered by how good it tasted. "As much as I wish the reason why I came back was different, it is kind of nice to be away from my regular life. I needed a breather from it. And it's good to be back in our hometown."

Hazel smiled and nodded. "I understand. Marriage is such a complicated thing. And it's always nice to come back home."

Alexis smiled back sympathetically, knowing Hazel was probably thinking about her short marriage to Simon, the boy she'd become engaged to at the end of high school. They'd moved out of Rosewood Beach together, but Hazel had returned after her marriage had fallen apart. "I know you understand. And I'm glad you've been able to make a home here in Rosewood Beach."

As she took another bite of her frittata, her heart thumped with worry. She could only hope that her own marriage wasn't going to end in divorce. Hazel seemed to suspect that her relationship with Grayson was getting rocky, but Alexis wasn't ready to admit out loud to her sister that she was having relationship issues. She felt embarrassed about it, and she didn't want to dwell on a painful subject, especially when the painful subject of their father's death couldn't be avoided.

Almost as if she'd read Alexis's thoughts, Hazel cleared her throat gently. Alexis knew from her sister's suddenly hesitant manner that she was about to bring up something related to the funeral.

"So, I told Mom I would make arrangements with the florist today," Hazel said. "I'm worried I'm going to start crying in the woman's office and be a total mess. Would you come along with me?"

"I'd be happy to," Alexis said, smiling at her. She reached over and squeezed her sister's hand. "That sounds like something we should do together."

CHAPTER SIX

"You have a good day today, okay, honey?" Cooper crouched down and looked his baby daughter Macey in the eyes. They were on the sidewalk outside of her daycare, early in the morning. "I'll be back really soon. You have fun with your friends, okay?"

"Okay, Daddy."

Macey still didn't know many words, and she spoke with the adorably sloppy diction of a toddler. "Okay, Daddy" was the phrase she said the most, and his heart still warmed every time he heard it.

He stood up, and Macey took the hand of the smiling daycare worker who was waiting to lead her inside the building.

"She's been doing really well," the young woman

said, looking down at Macey with kind eyes. "She's got lots of friends to play with here."

"Glad to hear it." Cooper smiled as he watched Macey and the daycare worker walk into the building together. Macey was babbling incoherently about something, although he thought he heard the words "chocolate milk."

He sighed as he turned around and headed back toward his truck. He hated dropping her off at daycare, but he was on a job that day that required him to leave the office for a while, and keeping her with him would have been impossible. Although he knew that dropping her off at daycare was necessary, he still struggled with feeling uncomfortable about it. He knew that sometimes she felt scared at the daycare and she missed him, and he wished that he could somehow be handling his single father situation better than he was. Sometimes he told himself he should get an entirely different job, one that would allow him to stay with Macey during the day, or perhaps he should get a job that paid better so he could afford a nanny—

He shook himself. He'd gone over these arguments with himself too many times already. Macey was doing well in daycare, and it was a great place where she could spend time with other kids her own age. He needed to stop doubting himself and focus on the workday ahead of him. Work was how he supported himself and Macey, and work was what he needed to do at the moment.

He was on his way to meet with a man named Judd McCormick, to discuss a landscaping job for a patch of land in Rosewood Beach. He typed the address that Judd had sent him into his GPS and made his way there.

This looks familiar, he thought as he approached the spot, and then he frowned in confusion.

He parked alongside the curb and then double-checked the address. He felt sure he must have come to the wrong spot, somehow. He was right where he had caught the beautiful woman wearing the high heels. In front of him was a cheerful-looking restaurant with a sign next to the front door that read, "The Lighthouse Grill."

He got out of his car, guessing that there must have been some mistake. This wasn't a spot for landscaping—the only greenery he could see belonged to the patches of grass placed along the sidewalk, and those belonged to the town.

"You must be Cooper Harris."

Cooper turned around and saw a stocky man striding toward him along the sidewalk. The man reached his hand out the moment he reached Cooper's side and offered him a handshake that was so firm it was almost uncomfortable.

"Judd McCormick," the man said. "Nice to meet you."

"You as well." Cooper smiled in a friendly manner, although he had to admit to himself that there was something about Judd that was off-putting. He was middle-aged and handsome, wearing a sleek business suit with a pair of sunglasses tucked into the front pocket. He gave off an energy like a bulldozer, strong and forceful, and Cooper got the impression that he was the kind of businessman who never let anything stand in his way. He guessed that Judd McCormick was both ambitious and ruthless, and the smile on his face looked as insincere as a smile painted on a cartoon advertisement.

"So, what do you think of the place?" Judd asked, turning to The Lighthouse Grill with a satisfied expression. "Nice spot, isn't it? Central to the town, as you can see. Obviously, there's not much room for landscaping now, but we plan to add all kinds of fancy additions when we have the land."

Cooper cleared his throat. "Have they already sold it to you? I don't see a 'for sale' sign anywhere."

"They haven't sold it to me yet, but they will."

Judd's painted-on smile widened. "I want this spot. My family has been cultivating McCormick's Brewery for many years. Two of my sons, Seth and Brady, work closely with me in the family business, and we've made quite a name for ourselves, producing beer to be bought in bulk. We're at the point where it's time for us to have a walk-in location, and that's where this new project comes in."

"Okay." Cooper didn't know what else to say. The wheels of his mind were turning, but he still didn't know what to make of Judd or the whole situation.

"I wanted to meet with you here today so you could get a look at the spot." Judd smiled. "Obviously, this whole porch for outdoor seating would be gone, which frees up a lot of space. There's also a green area in the back of the restaurant which you can't see from the street. It overlooks the water. It's a great spot. What would you recommend in the way of landscaping? You know, in order to turn the place into an attractive and functional location?"

"Assuming the purchase of land happens?"

"Oh, it will. What kind of an estimate can you give me on that?"

Cooper nodded hesitantly, still unsure as to why Judd took it for granted that the sale of land was going to happen. "Well, I can give you an idea of the estimate for the landscaping, but as far as the purchase of the land goes, that's out of my scope."

"I'm sure everything will be squared away easily as far as that goes." Judd's smile was complacent. "Just give me an estimate on the landscaping. We want some gardens, some bushes, good turf, that kind of thing." For a few minutes, he described in detail what he wanted in regard to the landscaping.

Cooper nodded as Judd went on and on. He took notes as he listened to Judd's plans, marking down all of the things Judd wanted, along with the quantities or approximate square footage. Once Judd had finished describing his goals for the place, Cooper used his list to quickly jot down an itemized estimate.

"That looks fine." Judd looked over the estimate, smiling. "Sounds like we have a deal here, Mr. Harris." He clapped Cooper's hand into another solid handshake, and Cooper nodded.

"Pleasure doing business with you, sir," he said, although he wasn't sure he meant it.

He and Judd talked for a few moments longer—Judd doing most of the talking—and then the men parted ways. Cooper got back inside his car, unable to shake the feeling that something was off about the whole thing.

Just before he turned his key in the ignition, he looked up at the sidewalk and lifted his eyebrows. It was her. The woman who he'd caught the other day in the rain, who'd wobbled as she was getting out of the taxi. The woman who had cost him his coffee, and then had stayed in his thoughts for the rest of the day.

She was walking toward the pub, just like she had been after getting her suitcase out of the taxi the other day. He wondered if she worked there—although he'd never seen a waitress wearing heels like that before.

She must have something to do with that place, if she showed up there with the taxi the other day and she's there again now, he thought, watching her step casually through the doorway with the familiar energy of a person who had done so a thousand times before. *Maybe she changes into different shoes once she's inside.*

He grunted with interest, and then realized he should get going. He turned his key in the ignition, deciding that he needed to make a point of going to The Lighthouse Grill for lunch sometime.

Julia pushed open the door of The Lighthouse

Grill and took a deep breath of the familiar smells.
Now that it wasn't her first time back inside since her
father's passing, she was able to enjoy the flood of
memories that surrounded her more. The Lighthouse
Grill had always felt like home to her, and she was
already starting to feel at ease there again.

She made her way across the dining area to one
of the booths, which was placed by a window
overlooking the water. Her mother was already
seated there, sipping a cup of coffee and looking
tired. In the next moment she looked up and saw her
daughter, and her face brightened with a smile.

"Hey, Mom." Julia sat down and reached across
the table to squeeze her mother's hands. "Good
morning."

"Good morning, sweetheart. How did you
sleep?"

"Oh, fine."

The truth was that she'd slept terribly, since her
mind had wanted to over-analyze and try to problem-
solve all of the problems that she couldn't actually
solve all night. But she still felt fairly refreshed, and
she had a feeling that being back in the clean air and
the slower pace of life of Rosewood Beach had
something to do with that.

"How did you sleep, Mom?"

"Oh, fine."

Julia smiled affectionately at her mother, guessing that she was lying just as much as Julia had been. She squeezed her mother's hand again.

"Thanks for arranging this. It'll be good to see everyone."

Vivian nodded. "It's important for us all to stick together as a family."

Julia smiled and then was quiet for a few moments. She felt a flutter of nervousness at the prospect of being reunited with her siblings. It had been so long since they'd really caught up, and she almost felt as though they were strangers to her now.

"We should get some menus on the table," she said, noticing that there were only glasses of water and rolls of silverware placed on it. She felt restless and she wanted to do something productive.

Vivian shook her head. "I already ordered for you kids. I remember exactly how you all like your breakfast burritos."

Julia smiled, touched by her mother's care for each of them. She didn't have the heart to mention to her mother that it was more than likely that some of their tastes had changed since they were last there together. Although she had to admit that she herself did still prefer her breakfast burritos the same way, with ham, hash browns, onions, red peppers, tomatoes, and plenty of cheese.

She poured herself a cup of coffee and added a splash of cream. She took a sip, savoring the taste. "Mm. Still the best coffee in town besides Ocean Breeze Café."

"Oh, I could never compete with Sally. But we do make a good roast here." Vivian smiled, looking pleased by her daughter's compliment.

"Hey!"

Julia turned around, and a grin spread across her face as she saw her siblings walking toward them.

Dean, with his messy dark brown hair and dark blue eyes, was flashing his crooked grin at them. He'd been quite the heartthrob in high school, and his shoulders were even broader now than they'd been back then. Ironically, he was currently single despite how many girls had wanted him back in the day— and Julia suspected that he still had his fair share of admirers.

"Sis!" he cried, opening his arms for a hug from her.

Laughing, she stood up and gave him a hug. Behind him, Alexis and Hazel were smiling at her, almost shyly, and she hugged them warmly as well.

"Gosh, look at us," Dean said, sliding into the

booth with as much charm and energy as he'd had as a kid. "We all grew up into a pretty handsome pack of animals, didn't we, Mom?"

Vivian shook her head, laughing. "Your father was so proud of all of you."

Instantly everyone got quiet. Julia noticed Hazel blink back a few tears, and her own heart felt suddenly heavy. It wasn't just that she was feeling the grief of her father's passing, it was also that he'd never said those words to her himself. Frank had been a quiet, hardworking man who was sometimes hard to read. She'd known he loved her very much, but he had seldom put his feelings into words.

"Come on, let's eat together." Alexis smiled at them all, clearly trying to lift people's spirits. "It'll be just like old times."

Hazel slid into the booth next to her twin, and Julia noticed that the old crackle of impish energy was still joining her and Dean. The two of them had always had a little bit of mischief up their sleeves, and some of their mutual pranks had been legendary.

"It's been so long since I've had a real breakfast like this." Dean leaned back in his seat, sighing with satisfaction. "I usually just devour a semi-frozen bagel on my way to the car shop."

Dean owned the local mechanic shop, Main

Street Auto. He'd gained a good reputation for being skilled, thorough, and fair in his prices.

"What? That's terrible. You need to eat." Hazel swatted her twin in the arm. "Come to our place for breakfast."

"I get up at six a.m."

"So do we, usually. Well, I do."

"I can absolutely recommend Hazel's breakfasts," Alexis said, smiling. "They're truly amazing."

Hazel flushed at the compliment, and Julia's heart warmed, seeing the camaraderie that was already returning between all of the siblings. They didn't feel like strangers to her in the slightest, and she felt a pleasant rush of relief.

In another few minutes, their breakfast burritos arrived, along with sides of extra hash browns and sausages. They ate hungrily for a while, everyone commenting on how good the food was. After a while, Hazel said softly, "I think we should share memories of Dad."

Alexis set down her coffee cup, looking almost wistful. "I agree. Who's got a favorite story of Dad?"

"Tell you what, I've got something that can help spark people's memories," Dean said, setting his phone down on the table. He began to tap at the screen. "I've got all kinds of scanned photographs here in a digital folder. I'm working on making a slideshow video for the funeral. We can all look at the pictures together, and you can help me decide which ones to put in the slideshow."

They all bent their heads down, looking at the pictures on Dean's phone as he scrolled through them one by one.

"Oh, I love that one." Alexis covered her mouth with her hand, laughing. "Do you remember that? There was that terrible thunderstorm, and none of us had any idea where Dad was. He finally came back, covered in mud, and all we could get out of him was, 'I tripped.'"

"We thought it was the funniest thing." Julia chuckled, remembering how silly their father had looked, covered from head to toe in mud. "We kept teasing him about being the gingerbread man."

"Oh, and look at this one!" Hazel leaned in closer to the screen, grinning over a picture of their father holding a massive trout in his hands. "That was the day I got so sad about him killing that fish so we could all eat it that he let it go. I think I was five or something."

"That sounds about right." Vivian laughed a little, although tears were glistening in her eyes. "I remember him saying, 'All we really need is the picture, as evidence.'"

The five of them continued to look through the old photographs, laughing and crying over them. They helped Dean choose which ones to use for the slideshow, and he scribbled down notes in a little notebook that Hazel lent him.

By the time everyone had finished eating, they'd reached the end of the pictures. Everyone was smiling a little, remembering their past with Frank fondly, except for Alexis. She looked pale and worn out, as if the grief had hit her harder than everyone else.

"What else needs to be done?" Julia asked. "I can help with more of the funeral arrangements, and I can help you sort through Dad's things, Mom."

She swallowed, knowing what a difficult task that would be for any of them, but especially for her mother.

"Oh, thank you for offering, sweetheart, but I know you'll need to get back to your job soon." Vivian smiled at her, her eyes still moist from crying over the pictures. "I know how busy it keeps you. I'm sure it's been hard for you to get away at all."

Julia's heart twisted, but she decided not to share

the truth with her mother just yet. "No, really, I'd like to help. What can I do?"

"Well, I do need some help sorting through the pub's finances. Your father always took care of that, and I've never had a great head for numbers. I'm dreading it a little bit, if I'm being perfectly honest."

Julia nodded without hesitation. She was great at math; it was something she'd always had a quick eye for and enjoyed doing. "Absolutely. You got it, Mom."

Reluctantly, they all started to get up, piling their plates and silverware together. Hazel and Dean picked up the dishes and started bringing them toward the kitchen together. Since they'd all grown up around the pub, they were used to helping out with the bussing.

Julia noticed Alexis hanging back slightly, looking as though she was in danger of starting to cry again. Julia felt concern for her sister, seeing how emotional she was. She knew that their dad's passing had hit them all hard, but Alexis seemed particularly fragile. She couldn't help wondering if something else was wrong.

CHAPTER SEVEN

Vivian slowly buttoned the front buttons of her sweater, standing in the center of her kitchen and staring into space. It was Saturday evening after dinner, and she was home alone.

Will I ever get used to this? She thought, looking around her cozy, tidy kitchen. *Being alone in the house like this?*

Frank had been a quiet man, and he'd often been gone at night, going out with friends or working late hours at the pub. But his presence had always seemed to be in the house with her, even when he wasn't home. She had never felt alone in their house, even after all of the kids had moved out, because if he wasn't there, she always knew he was coming back soon.

She took a deep breath as she finished buttoning her sweater. She contemplated getting a dog, or some other kind of pet, to help keep her from feeling too lonely. She smiled quietly, reminding herself that the kids were there with her. She could handle the days ahead with them at her side.

She wasn't looking forward to the task ahead of her, but she squared her shoulders and made her way to Frank's little home office, which was located just past the stairs. The room was small, little more than a glorified closet, but it had been packed full of papers. Frank had seemed to have everything loosely organized, but what had probably made sense in his mind was a puzzle to her. She'd already spent hours combing through the papers, making sure Julia would have everything she needed in order to put the finances of the pub in order.

She put her hands on her hips as she looked down at the desk. She only had one more drawer left to organize and clean out, and she told herself firmly that she could do it. It wasn't the cleaning that bothered her, but she seemed to feel the weight of Frank's passing so much more when she was sitting there combing through all of the papers that he'd arranged. He was never going to arrange them again, and she couldn't help being sad that she was pulling apart something he'd made.

She pulled open the last drawer and tugged out a thick stack of papers. Most of them were tucked into paper folders, but many of them were stacked loosely, or even crumbled. She set the stack of papers down on the desk in front of her, and then sat down in Frank's creaky old chair.

She began to go through the papers one by one. Many of them were documents that Julia should have, and many of them were old business letters that she put onto the trash pile she'd been making. After a few minutes, she came across a letter that made her frown. It was from a Judd McCormick, offering to buy the property where the pub was located.

"That skunk," she muttered, remembering the tall, smooth-talking businessman. He'd talked to her in person at the pub a few times, probably trying to sweeten her up. She'd found him to be disconcertingly insincere, and he'd seemed like the kind to only pretend to listen while in reality he was just following whatever narrative he had going on in his head.

She glanced at the date on the letter, and her eyebrows rose. It was dated the year before, a few years after Judd had come into the pub and spoken to her. She turned to the next document, and sure enough, it was another letter from Judd, dated the year before. She lifted up that letter and found yet another one underneath it. One by one, she uncovered several letters from Judd McCormick, all dated a year apart.

She shook her head as she read over the letters. They were worded almost exactly the same way each time. The man had clearly been determined not to quit, and she felt grateful that Frank had never given into him.

I still have the pub, thanks to you, Frank, she thought, taking a deep breath and feeling a bittersweet ache in her chest. *It's all the legacy I have left of you, aside from our children.*

Her heart lifted at the thought of her children. She didn't know what she would do without them there with her, and she wished that they could all stay a little longer.

Smiling a little to herself, she placed the letters from Judd onto the top of the trash pile and began to finish the rest of her work.

Cooper tried to stifle a massive yawn, but it spread across his face anyway. Behind him in the back seat of the car, Macey was finally sleeping, and he let out a sigh of relief.

It had been a rough night. His little girl had been restless and fitful almost the whole night, acting irritable in a way he didn't understand or know how to deal with. He was grateful it was the weekend instead of a workday, because he'd gotten three hours of sleep at best. He felt like a walking zombie, and Macey also seemed tired and still irritable.

He'd decided to treat them both to a fun breakfast out on the town, and they were on their way to The Salty Spoon, one of Rosewood Beach's local restaurants. Getting Macey ready had been a struggle, and he was beginning to doubt that going out to eat was a good idea. He wasn't sure how their outing was going to go, or how she was going to behave inside a loud, busy restaurant.

He a'rived at the restaurant and parked along the street outside. He could already see that their parking lot was packed, and he decided that he might as well skip the chaos and park there on the road. He glanced at Macey in the rearview mirror again. She was sleeping fitfully, but at least she was still sleeping, and he didn't want to wake her. He let out another massive yawn, deciding to take a short nap himself in the driver's seat. He figured they could both get some shuteye for a while, and she would wake him up when she'd awoken.

Feeling relieved at the prospect of getting a little more sleep, he closed his heavy eyelids and began to drift off almost instantly. In the next moment, however, a car horn honked loudly nearby, and Macey began to cry.

He forced his eyes open and turned around toward his daughter, speaking to her soothingly and patting her knee.

"It's okay, Macey, it's just a car," he said. "Look, we're here at the restaurant. You want to go inside?"

She made some kind of noise and moved her head up and down, and he took that as a "yes."

"Come on," he said, smiling at her cheerfully. "We're going to get some pancakes. You love pancakes, right? And chocolate milk?"

At the mention of chocolate milk and pancakes, Macey brightened. Cooper got out of the car and helped her out of her car seat, and then they made their way inside the restaurant together, holding hands.

The place was packed. People were talking and laughing and clinking their dishes, and waitresses and waiters were zipping around, hurrying from table to table. The place smelled incredible, but Macey took a step back, looking nervous.

"You want to go in?" he asked her.

She hesitated for a moment, and then seemed to remember the chocolate milk and pancakes and nodded.

He stepped up to the hostess. "Can you squeeze us in anywhere?"

"Sorry, it's a twenty-minute wait." She looked sympathetically at Macey, who still looked wary and cranky. "But I can give her some crayons to play with in the meantime."

His stomach grumbled, and he kicked himself for not thinking to make a reservation. "That would be great, thank you so much."

"Of course." The hostess smiled at him and took down his name for the wait list.

He sat down with Macey on one of the benches placed by the front door. She kept trying to get off the bench and walk into the restaurant, not understanding why they were waiting there. After her fourth attempt to go into the dining room, she was starting to get very frustrated.

"Not too much longer, honey." He smiled at her, hoping to help her feel calmer. "You want to play with the crayons?"

At first, Macey wasn't interested in the crayons or the disposable coloring-page kids' menu that had come with them, but he started to draw something on the back of the menu and that caught her attention. She was soon scribbling away happily, seeming to just be enjoying the way the crayons traced color across the page.

Cooper leaned his head back against the wall and felt his eyes become droopy with fatigue again. He glanced at his watch and sighed, seeing that they still had another sixteen minutes to wait.

It didn't take long for Macey to cover her whole menu—and some of the bench they were sitting on—with crayon marks.

"That looks wonderful," he told her, hoping the hostess would be willing to give them a second menu. She wasn't at the door at the moment, however, and Macey slid off the bench and started toward the dining room again.

"No, honey." He hurried to take her hand, but she tugged herself away from his grasp. "We have to wait."

"No." She frowned, her bottom lip starting to tremble. He could sense a tantrum coming on, and he took a deep breath, wondering what to do.

"I'm going to tell you a story."

She pointed to the dining room.

"It's a very special story. I can only tell it to you if we're sitting on the bench, and we have to hear it before we eat our breakfast."

Macey wrinkled her nose for a moment, but she loved stories, so she reluctantly toddled back to the bench. Breathing a sigh of relief, he took her onto his lap and told her the story of one of his favorite movies, substituting fruits and vegetables for the heroes, and moldy bread for the villain. He was able to coax a few smiles out of Macey, but a story like that would normally have her practically falling over with giggles.

When he finished the story, she glanced toward the dining room again and squirmed on his lap. He knew that twenty minutes must seem like hours to a two-year-old, and he glanced at his watch again. They still had a few minutes left to wait. Macey, sensing the release in his grip around her, started to wiggle off his lap toward the dining room.

"No, sweetheart. Not yet, we—"

He could see her face starting to scrunch up as she got ready to burst into tears. He winced, but at that moment the hostess stepped up to them. "All right, you two, thanks for waiting. We've got that table all ready for you."

"You here that, Macey?" He picked his daughter up, smiling at her. "We get to eat now."

Macey's tears evaporated at the prospect of food, and he breathed a sigh of relief. They followed the waitress into the dining room, where they were seated at a booth next to a window.

They ordered their food, and everything was going well for a while. Macey got a new kids' menu to color on, and their drinks arrived after a couple of minutes. Cooper took a sip of his coffee gratefully, and Macey wiggled in her chair with excitement as she took a sip of her chocolate milk.

Things stopped going well when she went back to coloring and moved her hand too wildly across her menu. She knocked her chocolate milk over, and the lid popped off. Chocolate milk splashed across the table in a sudden river and began to drip onto the floor.

Macey burst into tears, and Cooper set his coffee cup down in a hurry.

"Oh, don't worry, it'll be okay!"

Cooper looked up in surprise as a woman hurried up to their table, immediately dabbing the spill with a stack of napkins. She moved quickly and efficiently, smiling encouragingly at Macey.

"We'll get you another one, don't worry. Excuse me." The woman stopped a passing waitress with a polite gesture. "Could we get another glass of chocolate milk for her? This one spilled."

"Of course." The waitress smiled and hurried away.

The woman turned back to the table, finishing cleaning up the spilled chocolate milk, and Cooper started to help her, still feeling surprised by the way she'd swooped in so quickly to their rescue. She turned to him, smiling, and his heart started to beat faster when he recognized the woman who he'd caught in the rain the other day.

"Oh, hello." She seemed slightly taken aback for a moment, as if remembering how rude she'd been to him, but then her smile returned.

"Hi." He blinked rapidly and then smiled back at her. This time she was the one helping him out when he was struggling. He felt a little uncomfortable, worried that he came across as someone who was failing at rocking the single parent situation, but he couldn't help feeling a little tickled by the circumstances.

Now we've even, he thought, suppressing a smile as he dabbed at the table with a napkin. *This is a good way of breaking the ice.*

He stole another glance at her as she piled the soggy napkins into a heap at the end of the table. It seemed strange to see someone dressed in such fancy big-city clothes cleaning up a table at a restaurant, but despite her high heels and pencil skirt, she was clearly comfortable with getting her hands dirty. The way she'd jumped right in to help made him think she wasn't as prissy as she'd first appeared.

"Thanks for helping us with this." He smiled at her, feeling as nervous as a schoolboy around her, since she was so pretty. Her makeup wasn't as elaborate as it had been the first day he'd met her, but she was still strikingly beautiful, and her dark hair was pulled back with a gleaming black hair clip.

"Of course. I know how quickly these kinds of things can happen in a restaurant."

He found himself buzzing with curiosity about her. Did that mean she was a waitress? She sure didn't dress like a waitress. "Can I ask your name?"

"Julia Owens." She reached her hand out and he shook it. Both of their palms were slightly sticky from the chocolate milk.

"Cooper Harris. Very pleased to meet you."

They shared a smile, and then she seemed to be about to leave the table.

"What brings you into town?" he asked hurriedly, hoping she'd stay and talk to him for a little while longer.

She hesitated, looking sad all of a sudden, which confused him.

"My father recently passed away." Her voice was soft but steady. "I'm here for the funeral."

He swallowed, his heart going out to her. "I'm so sorry to hear that. My condolences."

She nodded. "Thank you."

"So your family lives here in Rosewood Beach?"

"Yes. My mother and two of my siblings live here, and another sister and I are back for now."

He liked the way she said "for now." It implied she wasn't about to disappear back to the big city. He found himself hoping that she wasn't going to.

"Well, we're glad you're back." He smiled at her, feeling a little tongue-tied and awkward. His heart was thumping in his chest as he wondered about her.

She flushed slightly, her hands resting delicately on the end of the table as if she wasn't sure what to do with them. She glanced at Macey, who had gone back to her drawing, and smiled hesitantly, as if she didn't have much experience with children.

"She's a cutie." Julia turned back to him, still looking slightly flushed.

"That she is." He glanced down at his daughter for a moment, fondness filling him, then returned his attention to Julia. "Do you... do you have any nieces or nephews?"

He'd been about to ask her if she had any children of her own, and then decided that was too forward. He glanced at her hands and noted that she wasn't wearing a wedding ring.

"I do, one niece. She's twelve now. I've been away so much it feels like she went from baby to pre-teen in the blink of an eye."

He chuckled. "Her mother probably feels the same way even though she was there the whole time. I can't believe how fast this little one is growing up."

Macey looked up and offered a chubby smile, seeming to be aware that she was being talked about. Cooper chuckled again.

"Are you here for breakfast?" he asked Julia, glancing around and wondering where her table was. They were fairly close to the door, in a large room, but he didn't see any empty tables or booths around them.

"That was my plan. Unfortunately, they're too busy here this morning. I'm happy they have the business, but it means I'll have to go somewhere else."

"I'm sorry to hear that—"

"Oh, don't worry. I'm on my way to The Lighthouse Grill anyway. It'll be easy for me to just grab some breakfast there."

"Oh, well, would—you can eat with us if you want." As soon as the words left his mouth, he worried that he'd been too forward. She immediately flushed a little bit and blinked a few times. "I mean, since there is nowhere to sit. Or you could join me—us—another time. Or..."

By that point, he felt sure that he was also flushed pink. He wanted to kick himself, realizing how sorely out of practice with flirtation he was.

"Thanks for offering," she said, smiling at him almost shyly. "But I've waited here long enough and I should get going. Besides, I don't want to skip the line, if you know what I mean?" She gestured back to where other people were still waiting for a table.

He felt disappointment flop in his stomach, although he had to admit her excuses were valid, and he liked that she was being considerate to the people in line behind her. "Of course. Well, I hope you have a good day."

"You as well." She hesitated for a moment, and then she smiled at him. "I hope I'll see you again."

"Likewise," he stammered, and she turned around and made her way toward the door of the restaurant. He watched her go, feeling his chest expand with hope.

CHAPTER EIGHT

Alexis listened to the sound of her sisters laughing and smiled. She took a sip of her lavender honey tea, feeling a cool breeze brush against her face through an open window.

She and Julia were at Hazel's house, and the three of them were sitting in the living room together, going through the rest of the old family photo albums. It had turned out that there were a few of them upstairs on a shelf in Vivian's house that Dean hadn't known about, so the sisters had volunteered to go through them together and pick out any photographs that they felt should be in the slideshow that Dean was making for their father's funeral.

Hazel had made them all mugs of tea, and Alexis found her beverage soothing and refreshing. It was fun to look at all of those memories with her sisters, but underneath it all was an undercurrent of grief, filling her chest with a bittersweet ache.

"Do you remember this Christmas?" Hazel pointed eagerly to a photograph of their dad dressed in a Santa costume. "He and Mom felt so bad about telling us that Santa wasn't real, and we were all like, 'We know.'"

Alexis threw her head back, laughing. "Oh, I'll never forget it. You remember how Mom was so worried we'd be sad that Santa Claus was really Dad that she baked all of those cookies?"

"Those cookies were really good." Julia laughed. "I just remember giggling so much with you guys because we felt so proud we'd already figured it out."

Alexis turned another page in the album she was combing through. In many ways, their task was easy, because they were only looking for photographs of their dad, and most of the pictures in the albums were just of them as kids. As she looked through the memories, she was reminded of how many times their dad actually hadn't been with them for various outings and events. She'd almost forgotten how busy he'd been, working hard at The Lighthouse Grill.

"And this day." Julia's eyes brimmed with tears as she held up a photograph of their dad holding a nine-year-old Dean in his arms. "Dean slipped on the ice and got that minor concussion. Dad was so worried about him."

Alexis wiped a few stray tears off her own face. "We were all so worried when we saw him fall like that."

For a moment, all three of the sisters were quiet. Alexis felt the bittersweet ache in her chest intensify for a few heartbeats.

As hard as this is, I'm so grateful we're doing it together, she thought. *And I'm glad I have some time to step away from L.A. so I can sort out my emotions about all of that better.*

She had been trying not to think too much about Grayson or her home life while she was in Rosewood Beach, because she knew that taking a break from brooding over how her marriage had been getting rocky would give her a clearer head about everything when she did finally go back. And she could feel her spirits being bolstered by the love of her family and the cheerful energy of Rosewood Beach. She wanted to drink that in as much as possible before she had to return to the things that were troubling her.

"How are you liking being back, Julia?" Hazel

asked, smiling at their other sister as she took a sip of her mango ginger tea. "Are you itching to get back to the hustle and bustle of New York City?"

Julia, who usually loved talking about her job and the big city, simply shrugged. She looked out the window and hesitated for a few moments before saying, "No, I'm not itching to get back."

"Well, they're probably itching for you to get back." Alexis smiled at her. "I'm glad they were able to spare you for this week."

Julia cleared her throat gently and said, "No, they can manage without me."

"Oh, I'm sure they're struggling hard." Hazel grinned at her. "You always said that they told you you're indispensable, right?"

Julia made a face and muttered dryly, "Well, clearly that's not true."

Confused, Alexis glanced at Hazel, wondering if she knew what Julia was talking about. But Hazel was staring back at her, looking just as confused as she was.

"It's really fun to be away from New York, actually," Julia said hurriedly, as if to try to brush off what she'd just said. "I'm really enjoying being back in Rosewood. It's been nice to be back in the quiet life for a while—everyone's so much more joyful out here, and our town is so beautiful."

"It is." Alexis smiled at her sister, but internally, she was still wondering what Julia's comment about not being indispensable at her job meant.

"And so much busier than it used to be!" Julia chattered on, smiling and seeming determined to keep the subject changed. "I went to The Salty Spoon this morning, and I couldn't even get a table before I had to leave to go to the pub. I'm glad tourism is increasing here, especially because that's good for Mom too. But the place was packed—I could have eaten there, I guess, but I didn't want to skip the other people in line."

"What do you mean?" Alexis asked curiously as Julia suddenly paused in her narrative.

"Oh, well, there was a little girl who spilled her chocolate milk so I hurried over to help do some damage control." Julia's cheeks started to flush slightly as she told that part of her story. "Her dad was very nice and he offered to let me sit with them, but I told him no."

"Oh, yeah?" Hazel set down her mug of tea, her eyes narrowing with affectionate suspicion. "Is this dad a single father by any chance?"

The flush on Julia's cheeks turned a deeper shade of pink. "I—well, I guess so. He isn't wearing a wedding ring or anything like that. And he seemed pretty worn out, even though he was being really sweet and patient with his daughter. I got the impression that he's a single father."

"Hmm, really. Is he handsome?" Hazel seemed all ears and determined to pry.

"I—well, I suppose so." Julia was decidedly blushing then. "Actually, I've already met him. The second I stepped out of my cab on my first day here, he caught me just as I was about to fall into a patch of mud."

"He caught you? In the rain? Oh, that's so romantic," Hazel cooed.

Julia shook her head firmly. "It's not—I was just being a klutz. And then I was rude to him. It was hardly romantic."

"Well, then today you got to help him out to return the favor. And he obviously likes you if he offered to let you sit with them."

"I think he was just being polite."

"Oh, come on! I'm sure he's at least somewhat interested. Men don't go catching random beautiful women in the rain without getting a few heart flutters about it."

Julia shook her head, laughing at Hazel's words. "Even if he was interested in me, that doesn't mean this is going anywhere. I mean, he had a two-year-old daughter and I don't know anything about children."

Alexis stayed out of her sisters' conversation, listening and smiling a little but not adding any input of her own. She did want Julia to find happiness with someone, but as she listened, she realized that she was feeling a little bit like a cynic. Given her own tense marriage, she wasn't in much of a positive mood when it came to anything romantic. She didn't feel as though it made sense to encourage Julia to get excited about some man who lived in another place than she did. However handsome he was, or however romantic it might be that he'd caught her when she stumbled in the rain, it was no reason for her to consider turning her life upside down for him.

"What do you think, Alexis?" Hazel asked, turning to her with a questioning gaze.

Alexis blinked. She hated to be the voice of pessimism, especially at a time when they could all use some cheering up, but she didn't want to be totally dishonest about her thoughts either.

She was saved from having to answer, however, because at that moment there was a knock on the door.

"Who would be knocking on your door after dinner?" Julia asked, frowning in surprise. "It can't be any kind of package delivery at this hour, can it?"

"Let's find out." Hazel stood up and hurried over to the door. The moment she opened it, the tips of her ears turned bright pink. "Jacob! Hi."

Jacob Dorsey, the town handyman, stood on Hazel's front step, smiling in a calm manner. "Hey, Hazel. How's your night going?"

Julia and Alexis exchanged a curious glance. Hazel had had a massive crush on Jacob in high school—she was one of many girls who had—and the sight of him showing up on her doorstep like that in such a friendly way made them raise their eyebrows.

"Are they going out?" Julia mouthed at Alexis, but Alexis just shrugged and shook her head, signaling that she had no idea.

She berated herself for not asking Hazel sooner if she had anyone special in her life at the moment. She told herself that it was her duty as a sister to know and care about those kinds of things. She realized she probably hadn't brought it up because she was avoiding the topic of romance as much as she could, since any reminder of her situation with Grayson made her stomach tense up.

"Um, fine," Hazel said a little breathlessly. "How about you, Jacob?"

"Oh, fine, fine." He smiled pleasantly. He'd always been a kind, down-to-earth sort of guy with a simple nature. He seemed to be blissfully unaware of how many women were still pining after him, even after high school. He was well-known enough in town that news of him had reached Alexis the other day at the pub, where she'd learned that he was now the local handyman, well-respected, and sought after by many women. She wasn't at all surprised, considering what a sweet, attractive young man he'd been when he went to school with Hazel and Dean. "I was just driving past and I heard a clicking sound coming from your fuse box."

"A clicking sound?" Hazel blinked worriedly. "That's probably bad, right? What do you think it could mean?"

Jacob shrugged good-naturedly and smiled at her. His kind gray eyes, along with his neatly-trimmed brown beard, gave him a professional appearance despite the fact that he was wearing a dirty flannel work shirt. "While I'm not formally an electrician, I know a lot about fuse boxes and I've done my share of work on some of the fuse boxes around town. I wouldn't worry about it—especially because I'd like to come by tomorrow and take a look at it for you." He grinned at her, and the flushed shade of her ears got brighter.

"Oh, would you? Thank you so much."

"Of course. I want to do my part to make sure everyone in our town stays safe. Call me if you notice anything odd happening before tomorrow."

"I will. Thank you again, Jacob. Get home safe."

"I will."

With a smile and a nod, he stepped off the front porch, and Hazel shut the door behind him, seeming to do it a touch reluctantly.

"Well, what was that?" Julia crowed gleefully, hugging one of the couch pillows to her chest and grinning at Hazel. "What's up with you and Jacob?"

"What?" Now Hazel's whole face was a bright shade of pink. "Didn't you hear him? He offered to help me because my fuse box is making clicking noises."

"Mm, yeah, I heard it. He really seems to be going out of his way for you, Hazel." Julia's eyes danced mischievously.

"But... he's just being nice." Hazel sat down in her spot on the couch and hurriedly drank some of her tea as if to hide her face.

"Oh, come on, Hazel, you had the biggest crush

on him when we were growing up. For years." Julia waggled her brows, poking her sister's shoulder with the pillow she was holding.

Hazel shook her head, although she looked as though she was trying not to smile.

"That doesn't mean he's interested in me! He could have his pick of any girl in town, easily. He's just being chivalrous." A silly smile formed on her face, however, giving away the fact that she was thrilled he was being so sweet to her.

"Ahh, look at that smile! You're totally smitten." Julia threw the pillow at Hazel, who dodged it, laughing.

Alexis swallowed, trying to fight off the pit in her stomach that wouldn't seem to go away. She was happy for her sisters, but the fact that their romantic lives seemed to be on the up-and-up and hers seemed to be plummeting to the depths made her heart feel as heavy as lead. She wished she could just enjoy her sisters' good news and exciting prospects, but their hope seemed to highlight the fact that she was starting to feel as though she didn't have any, at least as far as her relationship with Grayson went.

I keep clinging to the hope that things are going to get better, she thought, taking another sip of her tea and watching Julia and Hazel laughing on the couch.

I keep pretending I'll never have to say anything to anyone about what's happening. I don't want to have to tell anyone. I'm afraid to tell anyone.

She bit her lip, finding it harder and harder to tell herself that things were going to turn out okay between her and her husband. He hadn't even returned the calls she'd made to him since she arrived in Rosewood Beach. He'd replied to her with short texts that contained supportive words, but texts were far from reassuring, especially when she was dealing with something as difficult as the death of a parent.

She found herself pulling her phone out of her pocket, checking it yet again to see if he'd called her or at least sent her another text. There was nothing, and she had to rapidly blink back a rush of tears. She couldn't understand him not thinking of her enough to at least send her a message every now and again. So far, he'd only replied to her when she'd been the one to reach out first. She couldn't help feeling that if he really cared about her, he'd be reaching out and asking her how she was doing and trying to make sure she was doing okay.

"Oh, we should get back to these photo albums," Julia said with a sigh, turning back to the one placed on the coffee table in front of her. "I almost don't want to. It's so much nicer to think ahead to the future than look back at the past. The past makes me sad right now."

Alexis swallowed, nodding without saying anything. She was worried her future was going to make her sad too.

CHAPTER NINE

Julia took a sip of her wine and tapped the back of her pen against her lips. She was curled up in bed, going over the stack of finance papers from the pub that her mother had given her. She liked math, and she hadn't expected to find the task too daunting, but a preliminary glance at all of the paperwork told her that she might be in for more of a rollercoaster than she'd bargained for.

"Let me see," she murmured, scribbling down a few figures in a notebook that was lying open on the sheets next to her. "What does that figure mean? Come on, Dad. These are pretty cryptic. You clearly weren't expecting to go anytime soon."

She bit her lip as tears sprang to her eyes again.

She blinked them back and forced herself to concentrate on her math.

For another few minutes, she did her best to analyze all the documents and the lists that her father had written up by hand, but her frown soon became deeper and deeper. She took another sip of wine as she continued to scribble down notes, trying to make sense of the discrepancies in the paperwork.

All of a sudden, she froze. For a few heartbeats, she stared down at the paperwork, unable to believe her eyes.

There were questionable transactions littered across the documents, and she was suddenly hit with a guess of what they might be. At first, she hadn't had any kind of idea what they were, but then she was hit with a hunch that she didn't like in the slightest. Her heart was beating faster with dismay, but she climbed out of bed and went to get her laptop from where it was resting on a chair by the window. She brought it back to bed with her and opened it, pressing her lips together.

A great deal of money had been given by her father to some place called The Silver Horseman, and when she searched that name online, she discovered that it was a casino.

"Oh, Dad, no," she whispered, feeling shock thump in her bloodstream with every heartbeat.

She searched for a few more of the names that had been written alongside the questionable transactions, and discovered three more casinos, all of which were close enough to Rosewood Beach that they could be driven to.

She clapped her hand to her mouth, taking a deep breath. It was clear to her that her father had been concealing a gambling habit, something that neither his wife nor any of his children knew anything about. Or at least she assumed her mother knew nothing about any of it—she felt sure Vivian would have said something about it before asking her to look over the pub's finances.

She leaned back against the pillows, feeling stunned. She stared down numbly at the papers for a few moments, her mind racing.

She gazed down at the papers, her heart thumping, and then she started to shake her head. She refused to believe it. There must be some other explanation. Some of the transactions were dated as far back as twenty-five years ago, which would mean that Frank had been out gambling during some of the long nights during her childhood when they all thought he was working late at The Lighthouse Grill.

She picked up the papers again, going over the numbers and hoping to find some other explanation. Maybe he invested in the casinos as businesses, or he was friends with someone who owned them and he leant them money...

But as she frantically tried to find some other explanation for what she was seeing in the finance records, she became more and more convinced against her will that her father had had a gambling problem. It became clear to her that a lot of the figures weren't payments, but debts.

Her heart sank. She laid the papers back down on the bedsheets, taking a deep breath to try to steady herself.

Even more than the disappointment and shock that she felt, this created a problem. His gambling debts appeared to be unresolved, which left a huge hole in the financial security of the pub.

Oh, I hope Mom knew about this, she thought, running her fingers through her hair.

There was a buzzing kind of heaviness in the pit of her stomach. She kept pouring over the financial documents, taking sips of wine as she went, for the next few minutes, but the more she looked, the more she became sure that her father had had a terrible gambling problem, and that most of his debts were still unresolved.

She took a deep breath, closing her eyes. She didn't want to have to tell Vivian. She hoped that her mother had known, or at least had an inkling, of what Frank had been doing with their money, but she was worried that her mother had had no more idea of it than she'd had, and that the news would break her heart all over again.

Julia stacked the papers slowly, telling herself that there would be a way out of their mess and that it was all going to turn out all right. Hopefully her mother already knew. Maybe there was even some other logical explanation that Julia hadn't thought of. Maybe Vivian already had some kind of plan.

She turned out the light and lay down in bed, shutting her eyes tightly. She was dreading telling her mother.

"Did you know about this, Mom?" she whispered, opening her eyes again. "Or did Dad hide this from all of us?"

Vivian traced her fingers along the edge of a photo frame, gazing down at the picture of Frank. It was their wedding photo, a picture of them standing side by side outside the church and smiling broadly.

His green eyes crinkled slightly at the corners, his face framed by the thick red hair that had started to thin into baldness in later years. She noticed how muscular he was in the picture and thought to herself with a smile that he'd still been fairly muscular even as an older man, despite his stomach softening a little.

He looked proud, she thought. Proud that he was marrying her, and confident In his ability to succeed. He'd just started The Lighthouse Grill a few months before their marriage, and he'd been on top of the world back then, sure that they would have everything they could ever want and more.

"I did have everything I could ever want, Frank," she whispered, blinking back tears. "I had you, and a good life with everything we needed. And I still have all of our beautiful children."

She took a shaky breath, telling herself she needed to steady her emotions and carry on with her work. She placed the photo inside a cardboard box— the last box that she needed to bring to the church before the funeral, which was in two days' time. She felt relieved at the prospect of being done with all of the funeral arrangements, but at the same time she was grateful that all of the preparations had kept her busy. She was worried that her grief was going to hit her that much harder if she slowed down for even a moment.

She was just picking up the box, about to take it out to her car, when she heard a knock on her front door.

Curious, she set the box down and went to open the door. People didn't knock on her door without warning hardly ever anymore. That was something that had been common before cell phones, but now even her neighbors usually sent her some sort of message before dropping by.

She opened the door and her eyebrows lifted in surprise when she saw Julia standing there. Her daughter looked tired, and clearly upset about something. Julia's face, normally decked out in an elaborate makeup job, was pale and there were dark circles under her eyes, as if she hadn't gotten much sleep.

"Julia!" Vivian reached out to give her daughter a hug. "Is everything all right?"

Julia took a deep breath and said, "Can we go sit down and talk for a little while?"

Vivian knew in that moment that everything was not all right, and her heart sank.

"Yes, of course." She smiled bravely at her daughter, even though her bloodstream had started to rush faster with nervousness. "Come on and sit down in the living room with me."

Julia stepped inside and they made their way into the cozy, tidy living room. Vivian watched Julia's eyes sweep around the room slowly, and she guessed that her daughter was remembering all of the good times they'd had together in that room. Christmases and birthdays and family movie nights, with all of them shouting and laughing and playing games and eating good food.

She sat down on the couch and took Julia's hands in hers as soon as her daughter sat down beside her. "Now tell me what's troubling you."

"Mom." Julia looked into her mother's eyes for a moment, and then looked down at the carpet. "There... I was going over the finances last night."

There was a long pause, and Vivian's heart started to pound.

"Is something wrong with the finances, honey?"

Julia looked back up into her mother's eyes. "You don't know, then?" she asked softly. "I was hoping that maybe you knew."

"Knew what?" She squeezed her daughter's hands. "Tell me, please."

Was there something wrong with the pub's finances? Were they in trouble somehow? If that was the case, she wasn't sure how she could cope with it. In the middle of her grief about Frank, she'd been leaning on the fact that she got to continue running The Lighthouse Grill and carrying on the family legacy.

"I looked at the pub's finances last night," Julia said slowly, squeezing her mother's hands back. "And I found some strange things." She paused for a moment, and Vivian's stomach lurched. She could tell from her daughter's body language that something was very wrong. "I found that Dad had a lot of debt. That... that the pub still has a lot of debt. A lot of debt to casinos."

Vivian's heart stopped for a moment. She stared at her daughter, unable to believe what she was hearing. "Casinos? But—but Frank never gambled."

The way Julia winced made it clear that Frank had gambled. And if he had debts, that would mean that he must have gambled a lot...

She took a deep breath, trying to steady herself even though her blood was rushing in her ears. "Tell me more. Are you sure he gambled?"

Julia nodded. "He did. He gambled a lot." Her voice was soft, and she winced again, seeming to know how much the news was hurting Vivian.

"When? Just recently, or—"

Julia shook her head. "For a long time. It looks like he'd been gambling for years."

Vivian covered her face with her hands, unable to stop the tears from coming. She could hardly believe it, but she had to. She knew Julia was not only careful but considerate, and that she never would have come to her with that information unless she'd been absolutely sure that it was true.

"How could he have kept this from me?" she said, her voice almost a whisper. Frank had been a quiet man, but she'd always believed that he shared everything with her. He'd usually had good spirits, often whistling and making jokes when he wasn't quietly working or thinking. She couldn't believe that for all those years, he'd been hiding such an ugly secret from her.

"So you had no idea?" Julia asked softly, wrapping an arm around her mother. "And none of my siblings had any idea either?"

Vivian shook her head, feeling as though the ground was unstable under her feet. She felt as though her whole perception of her husband as the caretaker of her and her children had been deflated. "No idea. He—he lied to me for all those years."

Julia held her mother tightly, almost rocking her back and forth a little. "Everyone makes mistakes. It doesn't mean he didn't love us. I know it hurts, but it doesn't erase all the good things he was either."

Vivian took a deep breath, closing her eyes and feeling comforted by her daughter's words. "You're right."

"We're all here for you, Mom. We love you. Everything's going to turn out okay. And I will be right here with you, helping you figure all this out."

Vivian nodded, taking a deep breath. She would stay strong for her children, and she knew they would stay strong for each other and for her. As hard a blow as the news was, she was grateful that she didn't have to face it alone.

CHAPTER TEN

Alexis stepped back, inspecting the way she'd arranged some picture frames on a side table at the church. She felt jittery, wanting everything to look just right. It was as if she was trying to handle her grief in that way, by arranging and rearranging things, hoping that a perfect arrangement would make her feel better about everything.

It was the day before the funeral, and she was at the church getting things ready. They'd already had a few bouquets of flowers arrive, and she found their aroma comforting. She'd never realized how pleasant it was to have something alive and beautiful, like the flowers, in a place where people had to grieve a death.

It was a cloudy, gloomy day, and rain had been

drizzling down ever since she'd awoken that morning. She'd driven to the church soon after breakfast and was starting to feel lonely in the large building. She hadn't turned on any lights, and the hallways and rooms were dim and shadowy.

She sighed, still dissatisfied with what she'd done with the picture frames and feeling that they were off-kilter somehow. She stepped away from the table, telling herself that she couldn't be too perfectionistic, since there were still many more things to be done.

She started back toward the kitchen, where they had boxes stored. She was planning on taking out the last box of picture frames and beginning to arrange those around the church lobby, when she saw Julia step inside the doors of the church.

Her sister was dressed in a black raincoat, dark jeans, and black heels. Her outfit seemed to be a mixture of business and casual, and her hair was pulled back into a messy bun with a clip. She didn't have any makeup on, which was uncharacteristic of her, and Alexis guessed that she was having a difficult morning.

Alexis stepped forward and gave her sister a warm hug. "Where's Mom?" she asked, looking over Julia's shoulder. "Wasn't she driving with you?"

Julia shook her head, looking tired. "She was

supposed to, but she's having a hard morning. I wanted to give her some extra time. I'm going to go back there and pick her up soon."

Alexis nodded sympathetically. "I can't even imagine what she's going through. The funeral is going to be difficult for all of us, but especially Mom, I'm sure."

"Especially when she found out things she shouldn't have to be thinking about during her husband's funeral," said Julia dryly, her dark eyebrows furrowed.

"What do you mean?" Alexis's stomach gave a lurch. There was something about Julia's tone that implied that something was seriously wrong.

At that moment, Dean stepped inside the church, carrying a massive bouquet in a green glass vase. "Hey, sisters." He smiled at them, although he was also looking tired. "Where should I put this bouquet from the Johnsons?"

"Uh, put it in the kitchen for now. Thank you, Dean. We'll figure out the floral arrangements later."

"Sure thing." He started toward the kitchen of the church, and Alexis immediately turned back to Julia.

"What do you mean, Julia? What things did Mom find out?"

"What?" Dean turned around in a hurry. "Did something happen?"

Julia sighed. "I'm sorry. I shouldn't have blurted that. You guys shouldn't have to know about this during the funeral either."

"What?" Alexis urged, feeling anxious. "Tell us."

Julia looked down, biting her lip for a moment. Alexis's stomach twisted with worry. Whatever it was that Julia was about to tell them, she had a feeling it was going to rock their world in a bad way.

"So, Dad had a habit that none of us knew about." Julia looked up, meeting her siblings' eyes. "He kept it hidden from Mom, and all of us. He gambled."

There was silence for a few seconds. Outside, a car passed in the rain.

"Well, a lot of people gamble sometimes, don't they?" Dean shrugged, trying to brush it off, although he looked troubled. "I mean, it's not really that big a deal, right?"

Julia shook her head. "It wasn't just sometimes. It was a lot. Often. Regularly. For years. I found record of all of his gambling debts in the pub's finances."

"Debts?" Alexis echoed, feeling as though she'd gotten the wind knocked out of her.

Julia nodded gravely. "And they're bad. The—well, Mom's in trouble. The pub is in trouble."

"Oh, no." Alexis couldn't stop the tears from falling then, and Dean wrapped his arms around her in a hug.

"I can't believe it," he murmured. "Dad kept that from all of us all those years? I can't believe he'd do that."

"I can't either—or I couldn't." Julia sighed. "I kept staring at that paperwork, hoping there was some other explanation. But there isn't."

"This—this means that he was out gambling on those nights when we thought he was working at the pub." Alexis's voice was shaking. "He didn't just keep things from us, he lied to us. And he left Mom with a legacy of trouble and debt instead of security."

Unexpectedly, she felt angry with her father, something she'd never felt before. He'd let them all down by not being the man they'd thought he was. She reminded herself that he hadn't meant to die and leave their mother with the debt or the trouble, but she still wished she could talk to him and tell him how she was feeling. She still loved him just as much as she always had, but she couldn't help feeling betrayed and stunned.

Dean shook his head firmly. "We'll figure this

out. We—we can't let our own feelings get in the way of supporting Mom. We need to be strong for her, and rally around each other."

"I agree." Julia wrapped her arms around both her siblings in a group hug. "We're going to figure this out together. We'll find some kind of solution."

"Agreed," Alexis said, although her heart was fluttering. She took a deep breath. "We're going to take care of Mom, and make sure that everything turns out all right."

Unexpectedly, she felt a wave of peace wash over her. She might not feel as though she had any power over the way her marriage was falling apart, but this she knew that they would be able to fix. Together, their family would band together and make sure that everything with the pub's finances turned out all right.

CHAPTER ELEVEN

Julia took a deep breath. Beside her, Hazel reached over and squeezed her hand. Hazel's wavy dark blonde hair was pulled back into a French twist, and she didn't quite look like herself. Julia squeezed her hand back. They were seated in the front row of the church, waiting for the funeral to begin. Vivian was still talking to some of their friends and family members near the casket, her eyes glistening with tears but a smile on her face.

Julia let her eyes roam around the room. Soft violin music was playing over the speakers and the tune sounded both nostalgic and sweet. She felt comforted by the presence of so many of their loved ones around them, but she knew that she and her siblings and their mom were all carrying the added weight of knowing about Frank's secret gambling habit. Her sadness was deeper because of that, and she knew her family felt the same way.

The service began. She and her siblings and Vivian cried and laughed as people shared memories of Frank and spoke about their sorrow over his passing. Music was played, and words were read aloud. Julia felt comforted by having other people sharing in her grief with her.

After the service, they carried the casket out to the graveyard behind the church. That was in many ways the hardest part, but when it was over, Julia felt a sense of relief. The gravestone they'd picked out for Frank was beautiful, and they laid a colorful floral wreath at the base of it.

When the service was finally over, everyone went back inside the church for the reception. There was a long table covered in food, since almost everyone attending the funeral had volunteered a delicious dish to share. The large room adjoining the kitchen was filled with round tables, where people sat and began to eat their food.

Julia made her way along the potluck line slowly. Everything smelled and looked incredible, but she had little interest in eating. She made herself a plate, taking small portions of mashed potatoes, green bean casserole, and seven-layer salad. When she reached the end of the line, instead of going to sit down at one of the tables, she looked around the room for her mother.

She caught sight of Vivian standing in a corner with Hazel. They were both holding plates of food as well, but neither of them seemed to be eating. She made her way across the room toward them and gave them both a sideways hugs with her free arm.

"How are you holding up, Mom?" she asked. Her mother looked pale, although she was standing tall and appeared to be calm. Her eyes were dry at the moment, but there were faint tear streaks still visible on her cheeks.

"It's all so difficult." Vivian took a deep breath. "I want to feel as though now that the funeral is over, things will get a little easier, but I think it will be the other way around."

Julia nodded, her heart aching for her mother. "I'm going to stay with you," she told her, squeezing her shoulder. "I'll stay here in Rosewood Beach and help you for as long as you need."

"Oh, no, Julia." Vivian shook her head. "You don't need to do that."

"You've got a job to go back to in the city," Hazel said, a look of surprise in her eyes. "Dean and I are already here in town. We can help Mom out. There's no reason for you to jeopardize your career."

Julia felt a sense of panic rising in her. She felt an urgent need to be useful, to do something constructive and be able to help. She knew that her mother and Hazel meant well, but being pushed away, back to New York, was the worst thing that could happen to her at the moment. She wanted to be there with her family, helping to make things right.

"I want to help," she insisted. She struggled to get the words out. She knew that to her mother and sister, her insistence didn't make any sense, but she had to say it. She knew that what she needed was to stay there in her hometown and help her family get through their crisis.

Hazel, always observant, cocked her head to one side slightly as if she'd realized that something was up with Julia. "But what about your job? Have they said they can spare you for that long?"

Julia found that she was starting to cry again. She took a deep breath, determined to hold herself together.

"Julia," her mother asked gently. "Is there something you haven't told us?"

A couple of the tears spilled out in spite of Julia's

best efforts. "I don't have a job," she said, her voice little more than a whisper. "I—I got fired just before I heard about Dad. There's no career for me to go back to. Nothing's in jeopardy."

Vivian and Hazel stared at her in stunned silence. She couldn't blame them for being shocked, but the fact that they weren't saying anything made her stomach twist with a feeling of shame all over again.

"So I can stay here." She swallowed. "I want to stay here."

"Honey, I'm so sorry." Vivian reached out and gave her daughter a hug. "You shouldn't have to be dealing with all of this at once. I'm so sorry."

"They must have been really stupid people if they fired you." Hazel's eyes gazed at her sympathetically.

Julia shook her head. "It's fine. It's just a job. Honestly, in a lot of ways the timing worked out well. It allows me to just focus on being here." She could tell that they felt bad for her and she wanted to brush it all aside so they could talk about something else. She wanted to change the subject as soon as possible, since she was in danger of really starting to cry. The truth was that it *was* all too much at once. The double whammy of losing her job and dealing with worrying about her mother and the family business made her feel as though she couldn't find solid footing in her life. She didn't know what the future was going to hold, and it all felt overwhelming.

"It will all be okay." Hazel reached out and gave her a hug, almost as if she could sense Julia's thoughts. "Everything's going to work out fine."

Julia nodded, smiling at her sister and feeling grateful for her support. For a while, the three of them stood together in companionable silence, slowly and half-heartedly eating their food. Although Julia still didn't feel hungry, the food was delicious and it helped steady her nerves and give her a renewed energy.

The reception continued, and many people came to talk to Vivian as well as Julia and her siblings, offering them support and condolences. After a while, Julia felt as though she needed a moment to herself. She was grateful for all of the people around them who were showing them love, but at the same time, having so many conversations in a row was beginning to feel too draining, especially when she felt as though she had so much to think about.

She waited for the end of a conversation with Vivian's next-door neighbors, and then she slipped quietly through the door that led into the kitchen. From there she made her way into the church lobby and out onto the sidewalk.

It was raining slightly, but she didn't mind. It felt like fitting weather for the day of her father's funeral. She stood underneath a tree outside the church, hugging her arms and staring up at the sky.

Everything's going to be all right, she told herself. *My family is here for me, and I'm here for my family. We're going to get through this together.*

But she couldn't stop the tears from falling anyway. As much as she tried to tell herself that everything was going to be okay, she felt frightened by the idea that she didn't know what was about to happen in her life.

Cooper whistled a little as he strolled down the sidewalk, a plastic bag swinging in his left hand. Inside the bag was his to-go lunch that he'd ordered from The Salty Spoon. It was a chicken sandwich, mashed potatoes with gravy, and coleslaw, and he'd ordered it once before and knew that it was going to be particularly delicious.

Even though it was raining a little, he was in good spirits. He hadn't gotten a great deal of sleep the night before, but he'd gotten more than he usually did, and that felt good. He felt full of hope for the future in a way he couldn't quite explain.

Although the day was damp, it wasn't overly cold, and he had the sleeves of his work shirt rolled up to the elbow. He was on his way back to work, enjoying the fresh, green smell of the spring wind, when he slowed down in his walking, looking ahead in surprise.

He saw Julia Owens standing outside the church under a tree. She was wearing a black dress with long sleeves, black nylons, and another pair of fancy heels. She was standing with her arms crossed, looking up at the sky. As he got closer to her, he could see tears on her cheeks and a pained grimace on her face, making it clear that she'd been crying.

His heart jolted with concern for her, and he hurried over to her side.

"Julia," he said softly, and she turned toward him in surprise.

"Oh." She wiped her face and smiled almost shyly at him. She blinked. "It's you."

"Hi." For a moment, he felt completely tongue-tied and had no idea what to say. Even though she'd been crying and her makeup was smeared a little, he thought she looked strikingly beautiful. Then he snapped out of it and asked the obvious question. "Are you all right?"

She shrugged, forcing a smile. "Oh, yes, I'm fine."

"Um." He cleared his throat. "I don't mean to be rude or anything, but you're clearly not. You're standing under a tree in the rain crying. There's got to be a reason for that."

"Well—it's—no, really, I'm fine. Thank you for being concerned for me."

"No need to be a hero," he said gently, smiling at her. He gestured to a stone bench that was placed underneath a nearby willow tree. "Would you sit there with me for a while and tell me what's upsetting you?"

"I—" For a moment, she frowned as if she was about to say no, then unexpectedly she smiled at him and nodded. "All right."

They walked across the lawn of the church and sat down under the willow tree, which offered an excellent shelter from the light rain. It was a hushed and half-hidden spot, almost a world of its own. It smelled fragrantly of the rain and the willow branches, and the wind gently rustled the leaves all around them.

"You can tell me what's going on," he said. "Is it about your father?"

She nodded, taking a deep breath. She wasn't looking directly at him, but her body was turned in his direction as she sat next to him on the bench. "It's my father's funeral today."

"Oh, I'm sorry." He felt a renewed rush of sympathy for her. "Do you need to get back?"

She shook her head. "No, not right away. It's the reception now, and I've already talked to everyone I know who's there. I just needed a moment to myself."

He fought off an impulse to take her hand. "It must have been a difficult day."

"Oh, it was." She let out a long sigh. "It's hard to see how sad my loved ones are on top of everything else. But in a lot of ways, it was beautiful and healing to hear everyone talk about my dad. But that's not really why I'm out here."

He waited, wondering if she was going to say more. He didn't want to pry too much, but he also wanted her to know that whatever it was, she was free to tell him.

"I just had a conversation with my family." Her voice was shaky, and she blinked a couple of times as she spoke. "I should have told them days ago, but I've been procrastinating it. I feel ashamed, and I don't want sympathy, and—" Her voice trailed off, and he leaned forward, concerned for her.

"What is it? You can tell me. I won't judge you."

"I—just before I came back here from New York, I lost my job. They claimed it was because of cutting my position, but it turned out that it was mostly because one of my coworkers lied about me behind my back and they never asked for any kind of proof or for my side of the story."

He sucked in his breath. "I'm sorry. That must really sting."

"It does. And my family kept saying, 'Wow, I can't believe they can spare you from work this whole time, I know you're really indispensable to them' and I was just keeping my mouth shut, wincing over how wrong they were."

He nodded, understanding how difficult her situation must be for her. "I'm so sorry. Did you like your job?"

"Oh, I—I mean, I was good at it. I was very good at it. And sometimes I was stressed, and I didn't have time for much else besides working, but I really thought I was moving up. I've been working hard at my career ever since finishing school. So in a lot of ways, it doesn't just feel like I lost my job. I feel like I've been climbing a mountain and somebody just hit me with a baseball bat and knocked me all the way back down to the bottom of it."

"Oh, I'm sure it's not that bad. You must have a very impressive resume. I bet you can get a wonderful job somewhere else." Inside, he felt a squirming urge to wish for her to get a new job there, in Rosewood Beach.

She gave him a weak but grateful smile. "Thank you. I don't even have the energy to think that far ahead right now. For now, I need to just focus on—well, supporting my family and The Lighthouse Grill."

He nodded sympathetically. "I almost ordered my lunch from there today. I've been wanting to check it out. But when I called, I heard that it was closed today. Now I understand why."

"Yeah, everyone from the pub is here at the funeral today." She offered him a sad smile. "We're like a family over there. And we're literally a family over there—my parents and my siblings and I have all had some part in working at the pub for years. Not so much anymore now that we're grown, but we were there a lot growing up. It really is the family business."

She sounded upset, as if more was grieving her than the fact that her father was no longer running

The Lighthouse Grill. He wondered if she felt sad because her family had decided to sell the pub after Frank Owens' passing. He remembered what Judd McCormick had said about he and his sons buying the pub, and he wondered if that's what she was thinking about. He didn't want to ask her, however, since he was there to cheer her up and he had a feeling that dwelling on the subject would only do the opposite.

She took a deep breath and then began to cry again, covering her face with her hands. He placed the palms of his hands on his knees, resisting the desire to give her a hug. He watched her with sympathy, thinking to himself that sitting there under a tree in a fancy black dress, even though she was crying, she looked beautiful.

"It will all be okay." His voice was soft, and he wished he could do more to help her feel better. "Would you like half my sandwich?" He held up his to-go bag, smiling at her.

She shook her head, returning his smile and wiping some of her tears away. "Thank you, but I'm all right. We have food at the reception."

"Yeah, but you barely ate in there, right? Too many people. Everyone's sad and most of them are looking at you and wanting to make sure you're okay.

I bet you're the kind of person that doesn't have an appetite under those circumstances."

For a moment, she blinked at him, looking surprised. Her reaction seemed to say that his guess was right, and he nudged her gently with his shoulder.

"Come on. I've got too much food in here for one person. Eat half my sandwich?"

She offered him a watery smile and nodded. "Okay."

Grinning, he opened his bag and took out the to-go box. He handed her half of the sandwich in a napkin, and she took it delicately.

"Thank you. You're being very kind to me." Her long, thin fingers held the sandwich perfectly still in mid-air for a moment, and then she took a small bite.

He shook his head. "People need to band together and support each other. People are good at that here in Rosewood Beach, and I'm determined to be a valuable member of this community."

She laughed a little through her first bite of the sandwich. "Well, I applaud your efforts."

"Why thank you. How's your sandwich?"

"It's good. The Salty Spoon?"

"Clearly you are a restaurant professional. It is indeed from The Salty Spoon."

She smiled, and then they were both quiet for a few moments, sitting side by side and munching their halves of the chicken sandwich.

"I know today is hard," he said softly after a while, and she turned to him. "It's all going to be hard for a while, and I'm so sorry you have to go through this. It's so difficult to handle these huge upheavals in our lives, but you just need to trust that there's good around the corner, waiting for you. Things are going to get better."

She nodded and looked straight ahead at the gently-swaying willow branches. A bird chirped cheerfully in a nearby tree.

"I know how you're feeling." He sighed, remembering his own battle with grief, which he was still struggling with. "My wife passed away recently, and very unexpectedly. I have to believe that there's some kind of redemption coming after the loss, and that things are going to be okay. I still haven't seen it fully, but I want to believe that there's something good coming. I have to believe that in order to get through it all."

She turned to him again, her eyes wide with sympathy. "I'm so sorry." He nodded, and she added, "Thank you. That's very good advice."

"I hope it helps you get through this. Let me know if there's anything else I can do."

"You've already given me half a sandwich and some very encouraging words. I don't think I could possibly ask for anything more." She laughed lightly and then added, "Honestly, thank you for your kindness. It means a great deal to me."

They looked inside each other's eyes for a moment, and he realized that his heart was thumping in his chest.

"I'm perfectly happy to help. You know, when I mentioned meeting up with you again—when we were at The Salty Spoon—even though I said it awkwardly, I meant it."

She shook her head, and his heart sank, thinking she was about to say no. "You didn't say it awkwardly." She hesitated, and then smiled at him. "I'd like that."

He grinned at her. "You would?" His heart jumped up and seemed to be running around in circles like a terrier puppy. "How about getting some ice cream with me on Friday afternoon? Macey will be in daycare then. We could go for a walk while we eat it?"

She nodded, offering him the first happy-looking

smile he'd seen from her that afternoon. "I would like that."

For a moment, all he could do was sit there and grin at her, and she smiled back at him.

"So." Her voice was soft, and there was something in her eyes that hadn't been there a few moments ago. "Friday afternoon."

"Friday afternoon." He nodded decisively, his grin widening.

They sat next to each other, finishing their sandwiches in silence for a while. Finally, he glanced at his watch.

"Ah, I should go." He stood up regretfully. "I've got to get back to work."

"No need to apologize." She stood up as well. "I should get back to the reception. Thank you again for the sandwich, and for... well, just thank you." She smiled at him, and his chest filled with butterflies.

He walked her back to the door of the church and watched as she slipped quietly inside. She gave him a wave from behind the glass doors, and then she disappeared around a corner.

He stood there, feeling dazed for a moment. A raindrop splashed across his ear, rousing him from his reverie. He turned and started to make his way toward work, his thoughts focused on his anticipation for Friday afternoon.

CHAPTER TWELVE

Vivian sighed as she leaned over and expertly wiped off a table with a damp rag. She was at The Lighthouse Grill, helping clean up after the lunch rush. Around her was the sound of the remaining customers talking and laughing, and she could faintly hear the sound of pots and pans being jostled around in the kitchen. The warm, savory aroma of French fries, clam chowder, and meatloaf filled the air. It was comforting, being there in the pub, a place that she'd spent countless afternoons in.

It was the day after Frank's funeral, and although she'd told herself it was best for her to not go into the pub that day, she had felt too restless and sad at home. She wanted something to do with her hands, to help get her mind off the disturbing news of

Frank's secret. As much as the grief of his passing was still weighing on her, the news that he had been gambling behind her back was worse for her mind, because it was difficult for her to not dwell on it and start to worry about what the future might hold.

Four people stood up from one of the remaining tables and started to walk out of the restaurant. They all had big smiles on their faces, and they continued to talk and laugh together until they'd disappeared through the front doors. Vivian felt glad that the pub was still a place where people could come together to have a good time.

For now, she thought, her heart twisting with worry. *What are we going to do about all these debts?*

She walked over to the table that had just been vacated and started to clear up the dishes. As she was walking toward the kitchen with stacks of plates in her hands, a man walked into The Lighthouse Grill.

He was wearing a suit, and for a moment, all that she registered was that she didn't like him, and he made her uncomfortable in some way. Then she recognized him in a flash. It was Judd McCormick, the man who had been trying so hard to buy The Lighthouse Grill from Frank for years.

"Hello there, Vivian." He smiled at her as if they were old friends. "How are you doing today?"

She blinked at him, wondering if he'd heard about Frank's death. "Well, my husband's funeral was yesterday, so I'm about as good as somebody can be under the circumstances."

"I am so sorry to hear that." He had an expression of sympathy on his face, but it looked so wooden and insincere that it was almost patronizing. "I'm sure it's very difficult running this place without him."

"We're managing fine," she said coolly, shifting her weight as some of the plates she was holding started to slide a little. "Now if you'll please excuse me, I should get these put away." She smiled politely at him and walked through the swinging doors into the kitchen.

She carried the dishes over to the sink, placing them alongside it. She stopped to talk to the teenager who was working the dishwashing shift that afternoon, lingering on purpose so that Judd would be gone by the time she went back out into the dining room.

When she'd finished chatting with her young employee, she stopped by the pub's office for a few minutes. There wasn't anything she needed to do there, but she was determined to wait long enough for Judd to give up on her and leave the restaurant.

The last thing she needed that day was to talk to that man.

For a while, she simply sat at the desk, looking out the window at the sunlight glinting on the ocean. She found the sight comforting and soothing, and her jangled nerves steadied a little. Finally, she glanced at the clock on the wall and sighed. She should get back to work. She had a restaurant to run, and Judd was surely gone by then. It had been almost fifteen minutes since she'd gone into the kitchen, and she had a feeling he'd had no intention of stopping there for lunch, only to talk to her.

She got another damp rag from the kitchen and went back out into the dining area. As soon as she stepped through the swinging doors, her heart sank. Judd was standing there smiling at her, still in the exact same spot he'd been in when she'd left him. For a moment she felt as though he was some kind of vulture, waiting patiently for his prey.

"Must be busy in the kitchen." He grinned at her in a way that was probably meant to be charming but came off simply as toothy.

"It's always busy here. It's one of the most popular places in town." She moved past him toward a table that still needed to be cleaned, and to her frustration he followed her there.

"Well, it's a great spot. The land is good, right on the lake, and the location is ideally central. You've had a great run here, Mrs. Owens, but things must be rough for you because of your husband's passing. I'd be only too happy to go through with the deal that I've proposed to your husband many times over the years."

Vivian swallowed. She had to admit to herself that she was in a vulnerable position, considering what Julia had recently discovered about the pub's precarious financial situation. Perhaps that was why she had been so anxious to avoid talking to Judd, since she knew that talking to him might convince her that she should consider his offer, now that her perception of her circumstances had changed.

She hesitated before replying to him. She knew that in theory, considering his offer was the wise thing to do, but her heart rebelled against the idea. She hated the idea of selling the pub's land to Judd McCormick and his sons for many reasons. Not only did she dislike him and how persistent he'd been in trying to buy the land, but she knew that he would tear down the pub if he bought it. She couldn't bear the thought of their beloved building being razed to the ground, disappearing forever.

At that moment, Julia walked inside the pub.

Vivian glanced at her, and saw her daughter frown the moment she laid eyes on Judd. She didn't know if Julia had ever met Judd before, but she guessed that Julia knew a businessman when she saw one. There was something about Judd's overly-confident demeanor that screamed, "I think I have all the power here."

"What's going on?" Julia asked, stepping up beside Vivian, almost protectively. She fixed her eyes coolly on Judd. "Is this guy bothering you, Mom?"

"No, not at all, not at all." Judd flashed his toothy smile again, but his eyes glittered coldly as if he was sizing Julia up. "Your mother and I were just having a pleasant conversation. I've had my eye on this land for years, and I was renewing my generous offer to take it off your hands."

"What?" Julia's eyes flashed. "We're not interested."

"Come on now, sweetheart." His smile became wider, but not any more sincere. "I'm giving you the best option that you have right now, and on a silver platter at that. Your other options are to keep on struggling with this place until it falls apart, or to sell it to someone who isn't going to give you as good of an offer. I want the land—someone else will just try to buy the building, and let's be honest, the building isn't worth that much. Especially when word gets out that the pub isn't doing so well financially. People won't realize that the finances aren't due to any lack of quality in the restaurant itself, but due to—well, how shall I put this? Lack of quality in the management, perhaps. Frank always meant well, though. I don't mean any offense there. He was a visionary—always looking ahead to a bright future. Sometimes that made him forget about the present a little too much."

Vivian's heart felt hot and then cold for a moment. Did Judd know about how Frank had damaged the finances of the pub? Her head spun. She didn't know how he possibly could have, since he and Frank had been far from friendly, but his words and the knowing glint in his eyes made it seem as though he knew all about what had been going on.

She looked at Judd's face, and the calm, plastic smile he was wearing. She wondered if he actually knew about Frank's gambling somehow, or if he had just somehow found out that Frank wasn't good with money. Whatever he seemed to know, the fact that he knew it made her feel flushed with embarrassment.

Beside her, Julia stepped forward confrontationally. Her eyes flashed angrily at Judd.

"Our finances are entirely under control. Frank Owens made this pub the most popular place in Rosewood Beach, and you have no right to come here the day after his funeral and throw shade onto his legacy. You clearly have no respect for those in mourning."

"Now, Miss, I—"

"No." She tapped her heel on the floor for emphasis. "Please leave."

For a moment, he hesitated, as if he was considering saying more, but then he smiled again and took a few steps toward the door. Before going through it, he turned and said, "You're right. My timing was off. I apologize. Maybe we can find more to agree on soon."

Julia opened her mouth, looking ready to retort, but he slipped through the front door of The Lighthouse Grill before she had a chance to respond.

"Oh, that man." Julia glared at the doorway. "How dare he—and I'm sure that he—ugh!"

"Don't fret, sweetheart." Vivian wrapped an arm around her daughter and laid her head down on her shoulder for a moment. "He's out of our hair."

"For now! He made it perfectly clear he wants to come back. It's like he won't take no for an answer."

"You don't know the half of it." Vivian sighed.

"What do you mean?"

"Come with me to the office. I'll show you something."

They made their way along a back hallway to Vivian's office, where they sat down on either side of the desk. It was quiet there, and Vivian took a deep breath, grateful to be away from the hustle and bustle for a moment.

"What do you have to show me, Mom? Has he tried to buy the pub before?"

"Not once but many times," Vivian sighed as she opened a drawer and took out all of Judd's offers to buy the pub. She laid them down in a stack in front of Julia, who frowned and started to read them. "I was going to throw them away, but then when I heard your news about the debt, I—well, I thought better of it."

Julia shook her head emphatically. "You're not thinking of selling to that man?"

"Oh, no, I—it just seemed foolish to throw them out. Just in case. Perhaps as a last resort." Her heart felt heavy as she said the words, even though her impulse to keep the papers had been only a half-formed idea. She hadn't spent any time seriously considering Judd's offer, and she still loathed the idea of selling the pub's land to him. But she knew that she was in trouble. She had never run the pub without Frank before, and never tried to take care of the finances all by herself. She wasn't sure she could do it, especially now that they were in trouble.

Julia shook her head at her mother, but the look in her eyes was gentle. She looked down and finished perusing the letters. Her frown became deeper and deeper the more she read. Finally, she tossed the stack to the side with a huff of dismay.

"He really wants this land, that's clear." Vivian sighed. "And the price is fair."

"No." Julia's voice was firm. "He wouldn't be paying for the way we would all feel if we lost this place. If you lost this place. He's pushy, but don't give into him. There's no reason to. I told you I would help you with all this, and I will."

Vivian smiled at her daughter for a moment, her heart warming with gratitude. "I know you can help me. You're amazing at this kind of thing. I'm so glad you're here with me." As soon as the words had left her mouth, she regretted saying them. Julia was only there still because she had lost her job, and Vivian didn't want to feel happy about her daughter's misfortune.

But Julia smiled at her and nodded. "I'm glad I'm

here too. All of this is so much more important to me than my job ever was."

Vivian placed a hand on her heart, touched by her daughter's words. She knew how much Julia's career mattered to her, so the fact that the family business meant even more to her meant a great deal to Vivian. For a few moments, both of them were quiet, lost in their own thoughts.

"You know," Vivian said softly, "if you ever want to talk about what happened at your job, I'm here to listen."

"Thanks, Mom." Julia smiled at her and then heaved a long sigh. "Oh, it just all feels so ugly in hindsight. People here in Rosewood Beach would never do that kind of thing. People are too cutthroat in the city, always looking out for themselves."

"What do you mean? What kind of things did they do?"

"I got lied about—there was a woman at my job back in New York who didn't like me and told my boss things about me that weren't true. I guess I could have been a better team player, but she took one little truth and then turned it into a whole big lie."

Vivian nodded sympathetically. "Deceit is usually like that. The truth gets twisted. Either because people's emotions are keeping them from seeing clearly, or because they're being devious on purpose."

"Yeah. I guess she was upset, but she must have known she was lying about me in this case. Anyway, my boss didn't ask for my side of the story and I got fired. I just... I feel so betrayed on top of everything else. I thought they respected me there."

Vivian pressed her lips together, feeling a wave of sadness for what her daughter had been through. "I'm so sorry, sweetheart. Don't let it make you feel like any less of a person. After all, there could have been all kinds of other things going on that you don't know about. Maybe it was more about budget cuts than they made it out to be. And besides, you don't want to work for people who would treat you like that. You know your worth, and I know your worth. You want to be somewhere where your employers know it too."

Julia smiled at her mother, and there was a light in her eyes that hadn't been there a moment before. "Thanks, Mom. You're right. That makes me feel better about everything."

"I'm glad, sweetheart. You can always talk to me, you know? No matter what."

Julia nodded and leaned forward to give her

mother a hug. Vivian's heart warmed, feeling glad that she could be strong for her daughter even while Julia was also being strong for her, supporting her in the midst of the bleak discovery of Frank's gambling habits.

"I know, Mom. Thank you."

"Of course. You know I'm always here for you."

Vivian held her daughter tightly, grateful that whatever was coming next, they were in it together.

CHAPTER THIRTEEN

Julia stepped back from the mirror, inspecting the way she'd done her hair. It was half-up, allowing a great deal of it to toss around her shoulders. Her blue eyes blinked back at her curiously. For whatever reason, she looked strange to herself today, as if she was changing into someone else. She seldom wore her hair down, but it was more than that. There was a new kind of energy in her body that she didn't recognize.

I guess this much upheaval will do that to a person, she thought with a wry smile. *Then again, I may just be sensing my nervousness.*

She was getting ready for her date with Cooper, and she'd been trying to stifle butterflies about it all day. Even though the man himself made her feel calm and at-ease, the prospect of going on a date with him filled her stomach with jitters and her mind with questions.

She stepped out of the bathroom, going to look for her mother. She was getting ready for her date in Vivian's house, which made her feel a little as though she was in high school again. She'd moved into her old room after the funeral, and although it felt a little odd to be staying in her childhood home again, in many ways it was comforting.

It was important to her that Vivian wasn't alone in the house while she was getting used to Frank not being there. Now that the funeral was over, Vivian had more time on her hands, and Julia didn't want her to be spending that time alone in an empty house.

She was making her way into the kitchen when the front doorbell rang. Her stomach immediately filled with butterflies, even though one quick glance at the clock told her that Cooper wouldn't be arriving for another half an hour.

She made her way to the front door, and as soon as she opened it, a grin appeared on her face.

"Well, well, well." She pursed her lips as she took in the sight of Hazel and Samantha. "A couple of traveling salesmen. Can I help you?"

"Sales ladies, thank you very much." Samantha grinned back at her, holding up a large Tupperware container. She stepped inside the house and Hazel followed her. "And what we have here is free. Cornbread muffins for Grandma."

"Oh, that's her favorite." Julia's heart was warmed by their thoughtfulness. "That's so sweet of you both."

"No problem at all. We love to cook and bake. And we want to make sure she has as little stress as possible in the days ahead." Hazel smiled, but there was a troubled look in her eyes. Julia could tell that her sister was still worried about the pub's finances, as she herself was. "We also made her this chicken casserole—I made it once before when she and Dad were over at our place for dinner, and I know she loves it."

"Well, I'm sure she'll be thrilled. And those muffins smell absolutely incredible." Julia smiled at her sister and her niece. "Let's go to the kitchen and get the casserole in the refrigerator."

The three of them started to troop toward the kitchen, and Julia caught Hazel eyeing her with a suspicious gleam in her eyes.

"You look really nice, Julia," Hazel said, smiling slyly. "What's the occasion?"

Julia gave her sister a look. "I dress like this all the time, and you know it." She gestured to her pencil skirt and light green blazer. "Almost all of my wardrobe is business attire."

"Yeah, but you don't usually wear light colors and I haven't seen your hair down like that in years." Hazel was grinning as they stepped inside the kitchen. "You're going on a date, aren't you?"

"A date?" Samantha squealed.

Julia leaned her head back and groaned. "Fine. Yes. I am going on a date."

"With chocolate milk guy?"

"Oh, please don't call him that."

"I knew it!" Hazel let out a crow of laughter as she set the casserole down on the counter with a triumphant plunk. "I knew he was going to ask you out."

"You're going on a date?" Samantha set down the Tupperware full of muffins and scampered over to Julia. "Today? Now?"

"Yeah, in a little bit." Julia couldn't help smiling over their enthusiasm, since it showed how much they cared about her. "We're going to go get some ice cream, I guess. And go for a walk."

"Give us the details," Hazel begged. "When did he ask you? We've been so busy with everything, I'm surprised he got a chance to ask you out."

"Well, he asked me out at the funeral, actually." Julia blushed a little as she remembered how sweet he'd been, giving her half his sandwich as they sat under the willow tree together. "I stepped out during the reception. I just needed a breather, time to process everything, you know? Or try to, anyway. And he came up to me and saw that I was crying, and then we sat down on a bench under a willow tree and talked for a while. Then he asked me out." She wondered if her eyes were shining as she talked about him. She couldn't help feeling a little giddy remembering the encounter, but she knew that if she let on how much she liked him, Hazel and Samantha would never leave her alone about it.

"Under a willow tree in the rain? That's so romantic." Samantha clasped her hands together, looking starstruck.

Julia laughed. "I guess it was. He's very kind, and I—well, I like that. But today is just one meet-up, it's not like we've decided to start dating or anything."

"Yeah, but who knows what's going to happen?" Hazel grinned at her. "You look positively radiant. You really like this guy, admit it."

"I am really excited." Julia felt herself blushing

again. "But I'm so nervous too. I've been hemming and hawing over what to wear for about an hour."

She remembered how much trouble she'd always had dressing for important business events and meetings, and she realized that she was having even more trouble dressing for her date with Cooper. She couldn't help smiling a little over the realization, since he was so much less intimidating than a room full of business people.

"Well, sounds like you need some sisterly advice." Hazel grinned as she opened the refrigerator and popped the casserole inside. "So far, you look like you're going to a job interview. Ditch the skirt."

Julia looked down. "But I like this skirt."

"I know you must have at least two pairs of jeans in your wardrobe, I've seen you wearing them. Wear those."

"Besides, if you're getting ice cream and going for a walk, you need comfortable shoes. It'll be hard to pair comfortable shoes with a pencil skirt." Samantha nodded sagely.

"Oh, I guess you're right." Julia sighed, but she couldn't help smiling. "I'll go get changed."

"And then let us help you pick out some jewelry!" Hazel called after her as she made her way back to her bedroom. "You should have some earrings and some kind of necklace."

Julia laughed as she shut the door to her room. It felt fun to have Hazel and Samantha there, helping her get ready. Their enthusiasm helped soothe some of her jitters.

She quickly got changed into a pair of black jeans and tugged a pair of comfortable flats out of her closet.

"Okay!" She opened the door to her room. "Come on, fairy godmothers, help me get ready for this date."

"Yay!" Samantha squealed excitedly and scampered into Julia's bedroom. She made a beeline for Julia's dresser, where Julia had previously set out all of her jewelry in neat little rows.

"I like this gold necklace." Samantha held up a gold necklace with multiple thin chains. "It looks elegant but not too fancy."

Hazel followed her daughter into Julia's room, grinning. "Wow, it's a blast from the past to see you in here again, Julia. And here we are, talking about boys again. I remember I was in that chair right there when I told you about my first crush."

"I can't believe you remember that." Julia laughed. "I remember talking with you in here late at night with Alexis, but I don't remember that part specifically."

"Well, it was my first crush, not yours." Hazel poked Julia's side playfully, and then glanced over at the necklace Samantha was still holding. "I agree. That one looks great. Pair it with those little gold studs."

Julia did feel a little bit like Cinderella being transformed for the ball as they handed her the necklace and the earrings. She put them on carefully, and then turned around in a circle as they applauded.

"Yup. Now you're perfect." Hazel's eyes were twinkling as she nodded in approval.

"You look really pretty, Aunt Julia." Samantha sighed dreamily as if Julia was actually wearing some kind of ballgown instead of jeans and a white t-shirt under one of her most casual blazers.

"Thank you both. You've helped me feel so much less nervous." Julia beamed at them.

"Why be nervous?" Hazel shook her head. "He likes you, you like him, you both like ice cream. Sounds like a perfect afternoon."

"Oh, Hazel, it's more complicated than that." Julia sighed. "I do like him, but—well, I'm worried about getting involved with someone here in town.

I'm here for now, but I live in New York. I may not have a job there anymore, but it's where I live. I can't see myself staying in Rosewood."

"Hey, you don't know what's going to happen." Hazel waved her hand through the air dismissively. "Besides, maybe he isn't planning on staying here either."

"It isn't just that. I'm having trouble picturing myself with someone who has a kid already. She's adorable, but—well, I'm worried that the fast-paced nature of my life would make that complicated."

"Don't get ahead of yourself, and don't overcomplicate things," Hazel said, sitting down on Julia's old twin-sized bed and smiling at her sister. "Just be in the moment. What will be, will be."

"Oh, I don't know if I can manage that." Julia sat down on the bed next to Hazel and groaned. "My brain is always thinking ahead and trying to make a plan."

Hazel put her hands on either side of Julia's head. "Shush, Julia's brain. Just enjoy the date."

Julia laughed. "Okay, okay. I'll do my best."

"You'll look into his beautiful eyes and feel so swoony that you won't be able to think about anything other than how thrilling it is to be spending time with him," Hazel said, pretending to swoon.

"How do you know his eyes are beautiful?" Julia felt herself blushing a little as she reflected that Cooper really did have wonderful eyes.

"Everyone's eyes are beautiful if you like them." Hazel clasped her hands over her chest, and Julia threw a pillow at her.

The doorbell rang, and all three of them exclaimed in excitement.

"That's him, right?" Samantha said, running up to the window and looking outside.

"You can't see the front door from here, silly," Hazel teased her. "Come on, let's go downstairs."

Julia's heart lifted up with excitement. She told herself that Hazel was right, and she shouldn't let herself get stressed out about the upcoming date. It was going to be a great time—just her and Cooper, getting to know each other and taking things easily.

The three of them scampered downstairs to the front door, and Julia smoothed her hair down before tugging it open.

The first thing she saw was Cooper standing there, smiling shyly at her, and her heart did a somersault. The next thing she saw made her mouth pop open in surprise. Next to Cooper, holding his hand, was his little girl Macey.

"Oh! Hi," she said, blinking in surprise. She felt

as though she'd been thrown a little bit of a curveball, since she distinctly remembered Cooper telling her that his little girl was going to be in daycare during their date.

"Hey, Julia." Cooper was still smiling, but he rolled his shoulders back a little, showing discomfort. "I wasn't able to bring Macey to daycare today, because she's got some sniffles. I'm sorry, I hope that's all right with you. I—well, I didn't want to cancel." He gave her a smile that she found so adorable that for a moment she forgot about everything else.

"I—oh, yes, that's absolutely fine." She crouched down and waved at the little girl, who smiled back shyly at her. The truth was that she was disappointed it wasn't going to be just her and Cooper on the date. She felt as though she didn't know how to handle children, and the idea of Macey coming along on the date with them made her jitters return in full force. She felt worried that she wouldn't be good with Macey and that Cooper would stop feeling interested in her.

"Hey, Macey," she said, smiling back at the little girl. She was determined to do her best to become more comfortable interacting with children. "Do you remember me?"

Macey shook her head, hiding behind Cooper's legs a little.

"Her hair is different today, Macey." Cooper looked down at his daughter fondly. "She was the lady in the restaurant who helped us clean up your chocolate milk."

Macey just blinked at Julia, who stood up with a smile.

"It's okay, I'm sure she'll remember me after today."

"I'm sure she will too. Your hair looks great, by the way."

Behind her in the house, Julia heard a delighted gasp that she felt sure had come from Samantha. Repressing a smile, she turned around and closed the door behind her, catching a brief glimpse of Hazel and Samantha ducking out of sight behind the couch.

"Thanks for coming to pick me up," she said, smiling at Cooper as they walked down the steps of the front porch toward his car. He looked nice, too, she thought. He was wearing a light blue dress shirt and jeans, and his dark brown wavy hair looked almost curly, making her guess that he'd applied some product to it.

"Of course," he said. "I'm sorry again about the

extra passenger. And I might as well warn you now, she's going to take up a lot of my attention on the date."

"Don't worry about it." She smiled at him, but she felt another flop of disappointment.

Cooper tucked Macey into her car seat in the back of his car, and then he and Julia sat down in the front seats. She felt a kind of buzzing feeling under her skin, which gave her a sense of excitement but also of nervousness. He turned the key in the ignition, which started the engine of the car and also turned on the radio.

"Do you mind?" He grimaced apologetically as a kid's song began to pour out of the car's speakers. "It helps her stay calm while we drive."

Julia laughed. "Oh, no worries. I haven't heard 'London Bridge is Falling Down' in years. This song is a classic."

He laughed, looking delighted by her joke. She clasped her hands in her lap and looked ahead out the window, feeling pleasantly surprised to discover that the kid's songs was lightening the mood and making her feel more at ease.

"Daddy, make the face!" Macey called out enthusiastically from the back seat. It was difficult to understand her words, but Cooper had no trouble understanding what she wanted. He dropped his jaw into a goofy surprised face, which was evidently supposed to be his reaction to the fact that London Bridge had fallen down.

As soon as Cooper had made the face, Macey collapsed in a fit of giggles, and Julia had to giggle herself. She was charmed by the way Cooper acted goofy for his daughter to keep her entertained. It was clear from the way he kept checking on her by glancing into the rearview mirror that he was an attentive, adoring father.

I'm so attracted to that, she realized, surprised. *Just like how I didn't expect to find his rough exterior so attractive, but I do. The way he interacts with his daughter is very attractive to me.*

As soon as she'd had the realization, however, her heart twisted with worry. Clearly, Macey was Cooper's whole world. As someone who'd never come close to having kids of her own, the idea of caring for a child all the time felt foreign to her. She didn't know how she could date someone who already had a kid.

She shook herself, telling herself firmly that she couldn't throw away all of her concerns about dating Cooper just because of how attractive he was to her and how considerate he was. Although she had to admit to herself that it had been a long time since she'd met a man as considerate as he was, she told herself that she would be able to find someone great who was in the same place that she was as far as kids went. That person wasn't Cooper, so she shouldn't let her heart get too carried away on this date.

Cooper drove them to a local ice cream parlor, where they parked and he got out a stroller for Macey.

"It's a beautiful day, isn't it?" He smiled at Julia as they walked up to the ice cream counter, which was built at a window so that customers could order their treats from the sidewalk. "That wind off the ocean is delightful."

"It is." She smiled shyly at him, completely forgetting her concerns for a moment, just as Hazel had predicted she would. He really did have wonderful eyes, she thought.

"What would you like? My treat."

"Thank you. Um." She paused to peruse the menu, which was posted on the wall outside the ice cream parlor. There were so many delicious options, and for a moment she felt sure she was going to take at least five minutes to decide. Then she saw that they offered a dish with one scoop of orange sherbet and one scoop of creamy vanilla ice cream, and she knew that was what she wanted.

"That was my favorite as a kid," she told Cooper after she'd placed her order. "I used to take little tiny scoops of both with my spoon so I got the perfect combination of flavors every time." She laughed, remembering. Although the ice cream parlor they were at was a new one that she'd never been to before, she'd gone to get ice cream with her family many times while she was growing up. For a moment, she missed her father terribly.

"Sounds brilliant." He grinned at her. "I've never tried those flavor combinations, but it seems like a perfect example of opposites going well together."

"I'll let you try some of mine, if you want. I still owe you for that sandwich."

He laughed, and then stepped up to the window to order himself a turtle sundae, and a vanilla ice cream cone for Macey.

Once they all had their treats, he turned to Julia with a smile. "I seem to remember promising you a walk. Want to walk along the ocean? There's a great sidewalk that goes just along the beach—well, I guess you know all about it." He laughed.

"I do." She grinned at him. "That sounds like the perfect spot. And we can walk there from here."

They set off along the sidewalk together, beginning to eat their ice cream. Cooper pushed the stroller with his elbows while he ate his turtle sundae, and Julia teased him, saying that she was impressed.

"Parenting gives you a whole new level of skills." He laughed. "I can do things now that I used to consider to be superhuman. Functioning on an abysmally small amount of sleep, for example."

She made a sympathetic face at him. "Well, it must be extra hard for you as a single parent."

He nodded, all of a sudden looking more tired. She wondered if he was missing his wife. "It really is. Macey's so worth all of it, but there are days when I feel like I can't manage it all by myself."

"I'm sure it must be very difficult. But if it makes you feel any better, I think you're doing an amazing job."

"That does make me feel better." He grinned and popped a spoonful of ice cream into his mouth. "Thank you."

She laughed, feeling butterflies in her stomach again. He was so charming, she couldn't help feeling delighted by him.

"Daddy!" Macey called from the front of the stroller, sounding upset.

"What's wrong, honey?" He stopped pushing the stroller and hurried around it, crouching down in front of his daughter.

Julia stepped forward and saw that Macey had ice cream dripping down all over her hands.

"Don't worry, Macey," she said. "You have fun licking that off, and then I have something to make your hands less sticky."

Macey hesitated, looking unsure and stressed, but Cooper said, "Come on, honey, lick it off. See?" He pretended to lick her hand, and she giggled. "Mm, wow. That's delicious."

Macey licked the ice cream off her hand, and then Cooper coached her through licking off the melted ice cream on her cone. Julia and Cooper sat down on a bench next to the stroller to finish their ice cream while Macey happily chomped on her ice cream cone.

"Done," she said at last, and held up her sticky fingers in concern.

"You're going to grow up to be quite the lady, Miss Macey," Julia said, smiling at her as she rummaged in her purse for a wet wipe towelette. "Most kids don't even think about their fingers being sticky."

She crouched down and wiped off Macey's

hands with the towelette. Macey held up her fingers again, smiling because they felt clean.

"Here," Cooper said after Julia had thrown away the towelette in a nearby trash can. He squirted a dollop of hand sanitizer into her palm. "I don't want you catching whatever is making her sniffle."

"Why thank you." She grinned at him, spreading the hand sanitizer across her hands. "We make a good team."

He nodded at her, grinning, and then for a moment he got a look in his eyes that made her heart start to beat a little faster.

"You're really good with kids." He smiled at her as they continued to walk. He'd finished his sundae while they were sitting on the bench, but she was still eating her orange sherbet and vanilla ice cream, and she found herself carefully combining the flavors in every spoonful, just like she had when she was a kid.

"Oh, gosh, I wouldn't say that." She blinked in surprise over his compliment. "I'm not used to kids at all. I have one niece, but I wasn't really around when she was little like this. Honestly, I expected to feel really awkward around Macey when you said she was going to be on this date with us."

"Well, you're not at all. And I know she seems

shy, but she definitely likes you. I can tell." He grinned at her, and she smiled back.

For a few more minutes, they walked along in silence. The wind off the ocean gently ruffled their hair, and the air was filled with the smell of the saltwater and of French fries being sold at a nearby food truck. The sun was shining like a golden orb in a clear blue sky, and Julia took a deep breath, feeling delighted by how beautiful it all was.

"New York can't beat this." She half-closed her eyes for a moment, feeling the wind on her face. "Spring in Rosewood Beach is incredible. And summer is even better."

"I'm looking forward to it." He smiled at her a little shyly. "Will you be here in the summer?"

"Oh—I—well, I don't know. I'm not thinking that far ahead yet. There are some things—well, I just want to be here with my family for now."

He nodded, although he looked a little disappointed. "I understand. How is your family doing after the funeral?"

"Oh, okay I guess. We're all supporting each other, so that's been a huge comfort. But unfortunately, Dad's death isn't the only thing we need to deal with right now."

She hesitated. She didn't want to tell Cooper

about her father's gambling debts, not without her mother's permission, but she decided that it would be okay to tell him about Judd McCormick's visit.

"This man came to the pub the other day," she continued. "Judd McCormick. Apparently, he's been offering to buy the land from my dad for years, and now he's pushing the same offer on my mom. She... well, she feels overwhelmed by everything and how complicated it is, and I'm worried she might cave and sell it to him. That would break her heart. The pub means so much to our family. It's always been something that brought us together."

Cooper nodded, listening intently to her as she spoke. "I know the guy you're talking about. He rubbed me the wrong way, but I couldn't really place my finger on why. Now I know it's because he was lying to me."

"Judd McCormick? Why?"

"Yeah, he had me do a whole landscaping estimate on the pub's land—your family's land. He was sure that your mom was going to sell the place to him and his sons. He kept telling me it was a sure thing, even when I saw that there were no 'for sale' signs and questioned him about it."

"Ugh, the nerve of that guy. That's—" She felt her blood boil with indignation over the fact that

Judd had gone as far as to get a landscaping estimate before the property had been sold to him. "I can't believe that."

"I mean, I can. He seems unusually sure of himself, doesn't he? I almost felt like he knew something that nobody else did."

Julia paused in her walking for a moment, and he turned to her concern.

"Are you okay?"

"Yes, it's... well, I kind of got that impression from him the other day too. I don't like how cocky he is about the whole thing."

"I can imagine. He clearly thinks he has this one in the bag, for whatever reason."

"Well, he doesn't." Frustrated, she ate a spoonful of her ice cream and realized that it was just vanilla. "I'm going to do everything in my power to help my mom. Judd McCormick doesn't have a snowman's chance on that beach in the middle of August."

He laughed. "That's the spirit! You seem like a very determined woman."

"Oh, I am." She took another spoonful of ice cream, half sherbet and half vanilla again this time. "I've been working hard and planning my life carefully ever since graduating from college. I've been climbing the ladder all the time, if you know what I mean." She looked out across the ocean as she spoke, reflecting on how quickly the past few years of her life had gone by. She'd made money and had a lot of good times, and been very proud of herself regularly, but in hindsight it was all a blur. She couldn't remember many moments in which she'd felt as content and at peace as she did just then, walking along the beach with Cooper.

"I'm very different from you." He smiled at her. "I believe in working hard, and I do, but I've never been one for trying to climb that ladder of success. I used to own a ranch in Colorado, and that was its own kind of circus. After my wife died, I sold the ranch and moved out here. I was looking for a quieter, simpler life somewhere where Macey could be around kids her own age and I could have more time to spend with her."

She smiled at him. "I think that's admirable. There's nothing wrong with living a simple life. People here in Rosewood Beach are definitely happier than most people in New York. It's just that a simple life isn't for me. I always want to keep moving and doing things."

"Well, you're doing something now in Rosewood Beach, helping your mom keep The Lighthouse

Grill. Is it okay that I hope that keeps you occupied for a while?"

She turned to him and saw that he was smiling at her shyly. "That's okay." She smiled shyly back at him.

They had slowed down in their walking until they'd stopped. For a moment, they just stood there, and her heart began to beat faster. She wondered if he was going to ask to see her again, even though she didn't know how long she was going to be in Rosewood Beach.

"Julia!"

Macey held up a little fist with a flower in it. Julia looked down at her and realized in a flash that the little girl had picked a flower on the side of the sidewalk and was offering it to her.

"Is that for me?" She crouched down and took the flower that Macey was handing her. "Wow, thank you so much." Her heart felt light and bubbly all of a sudden. She hadn't expected to feel so touched by the gift of a flower from the little girl.

Macey pointed to Julia's hair, and she took the hint and tucked the flower behind her ear. Macey gave her a chubby smile, and Julia looked up to see Cooper watching the two of them with a grin on his face.

"I told you she likes you," he observed.

"I like her too." Julia smiled and adjusted the flower behind her ear.

They continued to walk along the beach for a while, and at one point they went down onto the sand itself and walked along the water's edge. Cooper left Macey's stroller in the sand and carried her, and Julia crossed her arms as she walked, wondering what it might be like to get to enjoy the beauty that was all around them on a regular basis.

"I had a really great time," she told him, when they were finally driving back up to Vivian's house. Macey was sound asleep in the back seat, her head lolled to one side and her tiny mouth open in a perfect "o."

"I did too." He parked the car in front of the house and looked right into her eyes. "I would really like to see you again, Julia. I know we're very different, and our lives are very different, and you don't know how long you're going to be here in town, but—"

"Yes," she blurted, and then she laughed. "I would like that. I'd like that very much."

"Great." His face lit up into a grin. "Next time we should do dinner. Or maybe go for another walk.

I don't know. I'd like to have a date with you where I can just focus on you."

She flushed, her heart beating a bit faster. "Having Macey along with us was fun," she assured him. "She's really a sweetheart."

They lingered over their goodbyes for another few moments, and he promised to call her. She slipped out of his car and made her way toward Vivian's house, feeling as light as a feather. She paused at the door and waved to him as he drove away.

I'm not going to let myself worry about this, she thought, unable to keep from smiling as she stepped inside the house. *I'm just going to be in the moment like Hazel suggested and enjoy getting to know Cooper better.*

CHAPTER FOURTEEN

Alexis shut her eyes tightly, willing herself to go back to sleep. Outside, she could hear birds beginning to chirp, heralding the dawn. She rolled over onto her stomach, as if that could soothe the way her brain was still going a mile a minute.

She heard faint plinking sounds and opened her eyes. It had started to rain, and droplets were beaded on her windowpane, catching the faint light of dawn. She looked at the clock on her bedside table again. It was five-sixteen in the morning.

She had been up for the past hour, worrying and fretting and grieving all kinds of things, but mostly her relationship with Grayson. She felt completely helpless but couldn't rid herself of a feeling that it was her fault somehow, and she needed to fix it in some way.

She rolled back onto her back and stared at the ceiling. There was that water stain again. She wondered if it was there because the roof leaked a little bit.

I just want my family to have everything they need, she thought. *But I know they won't accept charity from me.*

And what if she asked Grayson for money for her family, and he turned her down? Her stomach twisted at the thought. He'd been so strangely unpredictable lately, she had no idea how he might react to that kind of question. He hadn't even flown out for her father's funeral, which still stung. She'd wanted to have him by her side for at least a day.

Finally she heaved a sigh, deciding there was no way she was going back to sleep. She slid out of bed, shivering slightly in the cool morning air. She grabbed a soft white shawl off the back of the armchair that was in her room and wrapped it around her shoulders.

She tiptoed downstairs to the kitchen, where she boiled a cup of water in a pot so that the tea kettle wouldn't whistle and wake up Hazel and Samantha. She chose a bag of lavender tea from the many options inside Hazel's tea cupboard and went to sit down on the couch by the window.

For a few minutes, she sat looking out at the rain and watching the pale gray dawn slowly start to illuminate the yard more and more. There was a maple tree just beyond the window, and its branches shook fitfully in the wind. She sipped her tea slowly, feeling soothed by its warmth and pleasant herbal flavor.

Finally, she pulled her phone out of her pocket and sighed. She hadn't gotten a chance to talk to Grayson since she'd arrived in Rosewood Beach. He'd called her back a few times, but she'd always missed his calls. They'd been playing phone tag and missing each other for days.

She knew he was busy with work, but she couldn't help wishing he would put more effort into contacting her. She wanted to hear his voice on the phone, even if it was only for a few minutes.

She'd sent him a text the night before, asking him how he was doing and saying she hoped they could talk on the phone together soon. He hadn't replied to it, and she didn't understand how he could not take just a few seconds to check in with her and reply.

Almost as if she'd summoned it with her

thoughts, her phone buzzed with a response from him.

GRAYSON: I'm   doing   okay, sweetheart. How are you holding up?

She held the phone tighter, her heart leaping up as if she was some teenager and a boy she liked was texting her for the first time. She calculated the time difference and realized that he must either be up very late or very early for work. But she knew that he was awake because he'd sent the text. She hesitated for a moment, and then dialed his number, unable to resist her desire to call him. It rang a few times, and then he picked up.

"Hey, sweetheart."

Her heart stopped and she felt flooded with relief. It was wonderful to hear his deep voice on the other line. She felt as though he was some kind of stranger, but she was aching to talk to him anyway.

"Hey, Grayson. How are you?"

"Oh, I'm okay. Up late working. This new merger is going to be the death of me. Sorry—I—I'm okay. How are you?"

"Oh, fine." She twisted the edge of the shawl in her fingertips. "I'm up early. I couldn't sleep."

There was a short pause, and then he said, "I'm sorry to hear that."

"It's all right. It's five a.m. here, so not too bad. How is work going otherwise?"

He heaved a long sigh, and she didn't know if it was because he didn't really want to talk about it, or because even the thought of work made him feel stressed. "It's going well. It's a lot of work, but we're coming out on top. But enough about me. How's your family doing?"

She swallowed, not sure how to answer him. She didn't want to tell him about what they'd learned about her father's gambling debts, and the fact that he'd kept it all a secret from her family for all those years. "They're sad. Doing all right considering, I suppose."

There was a short pause, and then he said, "I'm glad to hear they're doing all right."

Their conversation felt strained and awkward. She felt a surge of sadness, realizing that there had been a time when she wouldn't have second-guessed what she could share with him. It was as though a distance had grown between them, and she felt nervous about trying to cross it.

"Thanks, honey." She swallowed, continuing to play with the edge of her shawl.

"How's everything else going? How's that little hometown of yours doing?"

She smiled wryly a little, even though he couldn't see her. Grayson had been to Rosewood Beach a few times before, and he'd never seemed to understand why she loved it so much. She knew he thought it was too provincial, at least for his personal tastes, and he liked the flashy, fast pace of L.A. He'd teased her about being a country bumpkin the first time he'd been to Rosewood Beach with her, and as she remembered that, her heart ached, realizing that it had been months since he'd teased her or joked with her about anything.

"Oh, it's good. Cute as ever."

"You're not homesick, huh?"

For a moment, she was confused, wondering why he would think she was homesick when she was at home. Then in a flash she realized that he meant homesick for their house in L.A., and the revelation that she didn't consider that to be her home made her feel stunned.

"Oh, I mean I am—"

"I knew it. You love Los Angeles as much as I do."

Her lips parted. She wanted to tell him that while yes, she liked Los Angeles, what she'd meant was that she was homesick for him, her husband. But the words died on her lips. She didn't feel she could say them, somehow—and she didn't know if it was because she felt shy, or because she was realizing that the emotional distance between them was becoming so great that the physical distance didn't even seem to matter. She felt more comfortable and at home there in Rosewood Beach than she did in their mansion.

"You're going to get back to our big beautiful house and wonder why you ever complained about your life here," Grayson continued.

She winced. She hadn't ever complained about her life in L.A., just expressed a kind of restlessness. Being the wife of a very wealthy man, with nothing to do besides go to yoga classes and design jewelry as a hobby, had made her feel as though her life was some kind of fraud, not any kind of existence she was meant to live. She'd felt as though she didn't have enough purpose. Grayson hadn't been able to understand that—he thought that by providing her with money and leisure time, he was giving her everything a woman could want.

Instead of responding verbally, she did her best to laugh convincingly. "I never meant to complain, honey, I—"

At that moment, in the background of the call, she heard a woman's voice. Instinctively, her whole body stiffened. She was about to ask him who it was when he interrupted her in a hurry.

"Alexis, I'm sorry, I have to go. I told you this merger was going to be the death of me. Talk soon. Love you. Bye."

He hung up, and she sat there blinking and feeling stunned. Her stomach twisted with worry. She told herself firmly that he was still at the office, and the woman she'd heard had been one of his employees, coming to tell him that something important had come up. That was why he'd hung up so abruptly, because he'd needed to put out some kind of fire relating to the merger.

She took a deep breath and then sat quietly, sipping her tea fretfully. By then it was cold, and not as comforting as it had been. She couldn't help feeling a little paranoid about what she'd just heard. Even though she told herself it was nothing to worry about, and she knew it was more than likely that he was at the office with other employees there, she couldn't help feeling anxious.

She sat and stared out the window, turning the situation over in her mind. It was so early in the morning for him, which made the presence of other workers seem odd. But he had said that the merger was going to be the death of him, so it was likely that his company was in the middle of some kind of "all hands on deck" situation. She told herself the female voice might even have been a message on his answering machine, and he'd started to get restless during their phone call and started to listen to it.

But no matter how many times she told herself that she had nothing to worry about, she couldn't help fretting. She shivered a little and wrapped the shawl tighter around her shoulders. She thought of how her father had managed to keep a secret from her mother for all those years. She didn't expect Grayson to be the kind of man to keep a secret from her, but she hadn't thought her father was that kind of man either, and he clearly had been.

She pressed her lips together, holding the sides of her mug tightly. Was it possible that Grayson was keeping something from her? Was he seeing another woman?

Her stomach did an anxious somersault, and she took a deep breath to steady her nerves.

I'm just jumping to conclusions, she told herself firmly. *I have no real evidence that he's doing anything of the kind.*

No matter what she told herself, she continued to feel heartsick and ill at ease. Even if Grayson wasn't having any kind of an affair, the reality was that he was slipping away from her. Something was tugging his heart in another direction, even if it was just his job instead of another woman. She felt a tear slip out of her eye and roll down her cheek. It splashed into her mug of tea.

She heard footsteps creaking down the staircase, and she hurriedly wiped the tears off her cheeks. Hazel appeared in the doorway a moment later, clearly concerned. Alexis realized that her sister must have seen her crying as she was coming down the stairs.

"Alexis, what's wrong?" Hazel hurried over to her side, looking worried. She was also still her in pajamas, and her hair was tied back in a messy braid.

Alexis shook her head, getting ready to tell Hazel that she was okay, and she was just crying about their dad, when all of a sudden, the tears started to come in full force. She couldn't stop them.

"So much is wrong." Alexis covered her face with her hands.

Cooing with concern, Hazel wrapped her arms around her sister and gave her a tight squeeze. "It'll be okay. Everything will work out fine."

Alexis shook her head, trying to blink back the tears. "I don't know that it will. I—I'm upset."

Her sister looked into Alexis's eyes for a moment,

and Alexis could see the wheels in Hazel's mind spinning. She got the impression that Hazel guessed that Alexis was talking about Grayson.

"Here." Hazel leaned over toward the coffee table, where she grabbed a box of tissues. She handed it to Alexis. "You take these. Take some deep breaths, and cry if you need to. I know just what this talk needs. I'll be right back."

Alexis offered her a watery smile, feeling grateful for her sister's care. Hazel smiled back at her and disappeared into the kitchen.

Alexis took deep breaths, dabbing at her tears with the tissues. The knot of anxiety in her stomach was starting to lessen, and she felt grateful that she was staying there with Hazel, who was so ready to comfort her. She knew she would have felt much worse if she'd been staying somewhere by herself, alone with her thoughts.

A few minutes later, Hazel reappeared in the living room, holding a tray of food. On it were two colorful plates covered in peanut butter and jelly muffins and bacon and egg bites. Besides the plates were steaming mugs of coffee. Both the food and the coffee let out incredible aromas, and Alexis breathed in the smells eagerly.

"There." Hazel set the tray down on the coffee

table in front of them. "I knew I was supposed to make these bacon and egg bites last night. This kind of conversation needs some tasty food. You take a few bites and then you tell me all about it."

Alexis nibbled her peanut butter and jelly muffin, enjoying how delicious the innovative flavor was. The food helped bolster her spirits, and she felt her anxiety dissipate even more. She felt overwhelmed by how sweet Hazel was being, and she hated the idea of telling her sister yet another sad thing.

After she'd eaten a couple of the savory egg bites, she set her plate down, her heart beating faster as she tried to brace herself for telling her sister what was on her mind.

"So." Hazel looked into her eyes, her expression sympathetic. "What's going on?"

Alexis picked up her coffee mug and took a sip, stalling. She felt she didn't have the courage to tell Hazel about Grayson, especially when she was being so sweet to her. "I—I just can't believe that Dad would keep that kind of secret from Mom. It's so jarring that he managed it—none of us thought he was the kind of person who would do that, you know?"

Hazel nodded, pressing her lips together. For a

few moments she looked out the window, seeming to be lost in thought. "We just have to accept the past, I guess. As much as it hurts right now. But I think we should be focusing on the present, and what we can do moving forward. The worst part about Dad's secret is that we still have to deal with it. It's not something we can forget about, because it's created this problem for the pub."

Alexis nodded in agreement. "You're right. We should focus on what we can do. We all need to think of ways to make sure Mom doesn't lose the restaurant."

"Yes." Hazel smiled at her, reaching over and squeezing her shoulder. "We'll band together over this. We should brainstorm ideas together."

Alexis smiled back. "Yes, we should." She took a sip of the rich, hot coffee that Hazel had brought her. She was feeling better about everything already, and she was glad to have something else to focus on.

CHAPTER FIFTEEN

"Oh, I can't wait to taste this." Julia grinned at Hazel, who stood beside her in line at Seaside Sweets Bakery. They'd met there to get bear claws, a pastry that had been a favorite of theirs during high school. Julia felt as enchanted by the cozy, sweet-smelling bakery as ever, and she couldn't believe how little it had changed since the last time she'd been there.

"Same. I'm lucky though—I get to come here and buy some whenever I want." Hazel elbowed Julia playfully in the arm, and Julia laughed.

"You've got me there. I've gotten some bear claws in New York, but they've never been as good as the ones here."

"Rosewood Beach is the best place on earth, I'm telling you." Hazel winked.

They stepped up to the counter and ordered their bear claws. Once they had them, wrapped in wax paper and tucked inside white paper bags, they strolled across the street to the grassy area in the town square. There was a cozy white gazebo there, and they made a beeline toward it. They sat together on one of the benches inside the gazebo, munching on their pastries and enjoying the feeling of the warm spring breeze.

"So..." Hazel drew out the word. "Tell me all about how your date with Cooper went."

"Well, you know about the first part! Honestly, I think you're setting a terrible example for Samantha, teaching her to eavesdrop like that," Julia teased her sister, referring to the way Hazel and Samantha had been spying on her and Cooper from behind the couch.

Hazel put on an expression of innocence. "I don't know what you're talking about. So. How was it having Macey along?"

Julia laughed. "It was really fun, actually. I mean, I am looking forward to spending time with him with just the two of us—"

"Oh, so there's a second date coming up, huh?"

"Shush and let me tell the story, will you?"

Hazel pretended to zip her lips but continued to smile.

Julia laughed again. "I was expecting to feel awkward around Macey, or not know how to handle helping take care of a kid. But everything went much better than I expected. I helped clean off her sticky fingers after we got ice cream, and then she gave me a flower. It was the sweetest thing."

"Oh!" cooed Hazel. "That's adorable."

"It really was. We had a great time together. She's such a cutie, and he's—well, he's very nice." She felt as though she might be blushing a little.

"Yeah?" Hazel asked slyly.

Julia cleared her throat. "So what about Jacob? He came over the other day to fix your fuse box, right?"

The second Julia mentioned Jacob's name, Hazel turned bright pink. "Yes, he did."

"Mmhmm?" Julia couldn't help acting a little gleeful. "Did you get a chance to talk with him while he was there?"

"Yeah—I—well, we talked a little. I brought him some lemonade while he was working. As a thank-you. Just to be nice."

"Girl." Julia shook her head, laughing. "Stop being embarrassed about the fact that you like him.

You're going to need to be a lot more obvious than lemonade if you want to encourage his attention."

"But I'm not trying to encourage anything," Hazel protested, turning an even deeper shade of pink. "At least, not right now. I just don't have the headspace for it, you know? Not with everything else going on. Mom's in so much distress over the whole gambling secret, and Alexis seems to be having a really hard time as well."

"I know what you mean." Julia sighed. "I don't really feel as though I have much of a bandwidth for my personal life either—well, that is until Cooper texts me or is talking to me, and then I can't seem to think about anything else."

Hazel grinned gleefully at her, and Julia winced as she laughed, wishing she hadn't confessed so much to her sister, who was bound to tease her about it.

"I guess that's even more motivation to get this whole Judd McCormick nonsense resolved," Hazel said. She took a bite out of her bear claw and munched on it thoughtfully. "I mean honestly, who does that guy think he is? Why is he so dang set on building a brewery right where our pub is?"

Julia shook her head. "He thinks he's someone important, that's for sure. But I have no idea why he's so determined. And I think he's wrong about the location being what makes our pub so popular. It's popular because it's a great restaurant. Mom and Dad built that reputation with hard work. That's not something he can buy."

"So true!" Hazel nodded emphatically. "And I don't know why he thinks that having a brewery take the place of the pub would really fly in Rosewood. People love The Lighthouse Grill, and they're going to be upset if it closes."

Julia's lips parted and she stared into space for a few heartbeats. She'd suddenly been struck by an idea, and she wanted to turn it over in her mind a few times before voicing it to her sister.

"What?" Hazel asked curiously, noticing Julia's expression.

"I just had an idea." Julia turned toward her sister, excitement blooming across her face. "What if we took a look around the existing branch of the brewery? Maybe that would give us a chance to see what all of the fuss is about."

Hazel's eyes widened. "I... yeah, I think that's a good idea." She grinned. "When should we go?"

"From what I've heard, they have multiple tours every day. How about we go right now?"

"Right now?" Hazel echoed in surprise. "But I have to get back to work soon."

"Oh, come on!" Julia tugged on her hand. "They won't even know you're gone."

Hazel wrinkled her nose. "Julia. I'm an administrative assistant at the doctor's office, they're definitely going to know if I'm gone. But..." She glanced at her watch, biting her lip. "I do still have some time. If we're quick, I can pull it off."

"That's the spirit!" Julia grinned, standing up and pulling Hazel to her feet. "Let's go to this brewery and check it out. Maybe then we'll have a better sense of what this is all about."

They hurried to Julia's car and climbed inside. The brewery was only a short drive from the town square, and they squinted at it in the afternoon sunlight as they approached.

"Mm. Pretty ugly." Hazel gazed up at the big cement building with raised eyebrows. "No wonder he wants our property."

Julia laughed as she parked. "Look, that sign says there's a tour starting right now. Perfect."

They hopped out of the car and made their way toward the entrance to the brewery.

"What if Judd is in here?" Hazel whispered as

they slipped inside the front door. "We don't exactly want him to know we're spying on him."

"Hmm, very true. Here. I'll pull up the hood of my jacket, and you pull up the hood of your hoodie. That'll keep our faces fairly hidden."

"I feel like a spy." Hazel laughed as she tugged up the hood of her comfortable light blue sweatshirt.

"We'll just have to do our best to blend in with the crowd and look inconspicuous."

The brewery was cool and echoed slightly. They slipped up to the back of the tour, which was just starting at the entrance to a long hallway. Julia peered around curiously, wondering if Judd was anywhere in sight. Then she realized with a jolt that Judd was the man leading the tour. Her eyebrows lifted in surprise —although she wasn't surprised by the extremely puffed-up attitude he clearly had about the brewery.

"Judd," she mouthed at Hazel, pointing toward the front of the tour.

Hazel nodded, mouthing back, "Ew."

Julia had to repress a giggle. They continued to follow the tour, staying at the back of the crowd, and gazing around the brewery with interest. They passed large silver vats as they walked, and the air was filled with a yeasty smell.

"No wonder they want our place if theirs smells like this," Hazel whispered, amusement in her tone.

"And it's so sparsely decorated," Julia whispered back. "White walls. All modern and without any kind of personality."

"If they take our spot by the ocean, they're going to have to make it another sit-down place. They'll have to serve food there, and I don't think they're up for that."

"I hope they don't think our chefs would be willing to work for them." Julia grinned. "We have the best chefs in town, but they would never agree to work for the enemy."

Both of them couldn't help giggling a little, but at that moment, Julia caught Judd frowning at them curiously, as if he was starting to recognize them. She froze, but in the next moment a tourist raised her hand with a question, unknowingly saving the day.

Julia glanced at Hazel and saw that she had also noticed Judd watching them.

"We should go," Hazel mouthed at her, and Julia nodded. She agreed that they should make themselves scarce before they could be fully detected —or worse, questioned by Judd.

They slipped out of the brewery and scampered across the parking lot to Julia's car.

"Well, all we really learned was that that place smells bad and it's boring," Hazel said, leaning back in her seat and laughing as Julia drove her car out of the parking lot.

"Yeah, but I'm glad we did it. It was an adventure." Julia grinned at her.

"So true. And I'm glad we left when we did, because I should be getting back to work anyway— oh, shoot! I left my water bottle in the gazebo. At least I think I did. Can you drop me off there? My car's right by there anyway."

"Of course! I'll come with you and help you look."

A few minutes later, Julia parked her car along the edge of the town square and she and Hazel got out and hurried toward the gazebo. They immediately found Hazel's lime green water bottle, sitting next to the bench that they'd eaten their bear claw on.

"Perfect." Hazel scooped it up. "I should get going. Thanks for being a spy with me, Julia."

Laughing quietly, the two of them descended the steps of the gazebo. A man was coming around the corner of it along the sidewalk, and they nearly collided with him.

"Oh!" Julia said, suddenly feeling flushed. "Hi, Cooper."

He was dressed in his work shirt, and his wavy hair was a little tousled by the wind. He had a lunchbox slung over his shoulder, implying that he was there on a meal break from work.

"Hey," he said, his face lighting up. "What brings you here?"

Julia immediately felt out of sorts, and she tucked a wisp of hair behind her ear. She felt wildly jittery all of a sudden, and she found herself wondering if she looked disheveled after her and Hazel's adventure.

"Hi," Hazel said, seeming to notice that Julia was feeling tongue-tied and swooping in to rescue her. She held out her hand and shook Cooper's firmly. "I'm Hazel, Julia's sister. I've heard a lot of great stuff about you."

"You have?" Cooper asked, brightening. He turned to Julia with a grin. "Why thank you."

Julia laughed, still feeling embarrassed but also delighted by him. "You're welcome."

"Can I ask why you both have your hoods up?" Cooper said, smiling with wry amusement. "You look like you've been up to something."

Hazel simply grinned unabashedly, but Julia

hurriedly pushed off her jacket hood. "We were—uh, we were just doing a little investigating in the interest of the family name."

"Hmm, sounds like a worthy cause." Cooper laughed, a rich, deep sound. At that moment, his phone began to ring in his pocket. He pulled it out, frowning. "Ah, I've got to take this. I'll see you soon?" He looked at Julia, his expression almost puppy-like.

"Sure." She smiled, still feeling flushed and flustered.

Cooper continued along the path as he answered the phone call, and Hazel and Julia walked back toward the road, where their cars were parked.

"Oh, I feel so stupid," Julia groaned under her breath as they walked along the sidewalk. "Cooper must think I'm nuts."

Hazel paused in her walking for a moment to give Julia a look. "Um, what? Did you not see the look on his face? He's completely smitten with you. Twitterpated. You have that very handsome, pleasant-looking man in the palm of your hand."

"Oh, I don't—"

"Shush. I love you. I have to leave for work now." Hazel grinned at her. "Talk to you later?"

"Talk to you later. Have a good day at work!"

The sisters hugged and Hazel hurried off to her

car. Julia walked to her own vehicle more slowly, turning over in her mind what Hazel had said.

Was Cooper really smitten with her? The idea made her heart start to thump in her chest. She felt so fluttery and nervous around him, but at the same time he made her feel comfortable in a way no one ever had before.

Could we have a future together? She wondered as she unlocked her car and slipped inside.

She sat in the driver's seat for a few minutes, looking out the windows and thinking. In the rearview mirror, she could see Cooper talking on the phone. She watched him, her heart fluttering, until he turned a corner and disappeared from view.

She wondered if she could ever leave her life in the city to be with a man like Cooper. Or would he ever consider moving to the city to be with her?

Her head spun with thoughts and happy imaginings as she drove along the streets of Rosewood Beach. She told herself that she didn't need to have all the answers yet—for right now, she could just let herself feel excited about getting to know him.

CHAPTER SIXTEEN

Cooper smiled to himself as he tossed a pile of dirty clothes into the washing machine. Ever since he'd run into Julia earlier that day, he hadn't been able to stop thinking about her.

His house was filled with the smell of a frozen pizza cooking in the oven for dinner. He always felt a little guilty about making "bachelor food" for meals, but he was also boiling a bunch of broccoli for him and Macey to eat along with their pizza. As he poured laundry detergent into the washing machine, he reminded himself that he needed to check on the broccoli in another few minutes. The last time he'd cooked broccoli he'd burnt it badly.

He started the load of wash, and the laundry room was filled with the sound of water rushing and the machine whirring. He thought to himself that it was like a mirror image of his mind, because there were so many colorful thoughts of Julia whirring and tumbling around inside of him.

He chuckled to himself, remembering how cute she'd looked, all guilty and skittish, and with her hood up. He wondered what she and Hazel had been up to, and he had a feeling that it had something to do with Judd McCormick.

Whatever it was, he felt sure that he was on their side. He knew they wouldn't do anything illegal, and trying to outsmart someone as slippery as Judd seemed like the sensible thing to do.

I admire her, he thought as he headed back toward the kitchen. *She's out of her element here, but she's still trying to support her family in a town where she feels a little bit like a fish out of water.*

He checked the broccoli and the pizza, and they were both done. Macey was playing with her toys on the carpet in the living room, and he paused to smile at her as he set the kitchen table for dinner. She looked happy, and he crossed his fingers, hoping that they would both get a decent amount of sleep that night.

He added a little cheddar cheese to the steamed broccoli, and then called to his daughter.

"Macey! It's time for dinner. I made your favorite vegetable."

"Yay!" Macey stood up and toddled into the kitchen, an excited smile on her face. "Cheese?"

He laughed. Macey despised broccoli on its own, but when he added cheese to it, she loved it. He decided to wait to correct her on the fact that the cheese wasn't actually the vegetable.

"Yes, with cheese." He picked her up, kissed her cheek, and placed her in her highchair.

All through the meal, he kept thinking about Julia. He was itching to talk with her, and he was wrestling with the idea of calling her on the phone. He didn't want to come on too strong too soon, but he told himself that they'd already been on a date and that calling her to talk for a while was a logical next step.

As soon as he'd gotten Macey ready for bed and tucked in, he hurried back to the kitchen, where his phone was resting on the counter. He hesitated for one more instant, his stomach churning with nervousness, and then he dialed Julia's number.

His heart thumped in his chest as he listened to it ring, and then he heard Julia's voice say, "Hello?" She sounded happy.

"Hey, Julia, this is Cooper."

"I know." She laughed breathlessly a little. "I have your number saved."

"Oh." He laughed too. "Of course. That's how cell phones work, isn't it?"

"Last time I checked."

He leaned against the counter, discovering that he had a huge grin on his face. "How's your night going?"

"Oh, fine. I'm feeling pretty tired. Just sitting here with some decaf coffee trying to read a little."

"Sounds nice. Are you tired after your sneaky visit to the McCormick place this afternoon?"

"You—how did you know that's what we were doing?"

He laughed. "I just figured. I know they have a lot of tours over there at the brewery. And honestly, it's what I'd do if I were in your shoes."

She chuckled. "Well, guilty as charged. We didn't get the full tour, though, since it seemed like Judd was starting to recognize us. He was leading the tour."

"He was? Huh. Guess he likes to brag about his company." He grinned.

"Oh, it definitely sounded that way."

"So you didn't learn anything valuable, huh?" He started to play with a magnet that was on the refrigerator, moving it back and forth, back and forth...

"No. I guess you probably thought it was pretty silly of us. Putting our hoods up like that as if it would really keep us from being recognized." She sounded nervous, as if she was worried that he thought she'd been foolish.

"Oh, not at all," he assured her hastily. "I thought it was cute."

As soon as the words were out of his mouth, he froze, no longer moving the magnet. He winced a little bit, wondering if it was too early for him to say something like that.

"Oh, you did, huh?" She sounded as though she was grinning. "Or is cute just the word you use for silly people?"

"No, cute is the word I use for cute people." He was grinning too. "I think what you're trying to do is very important, and anything that can help you achieve it is a good idea."

"Even putting up my hood?"

"Oh, definitely that."

She laughed, and he grinned, thinking to himself how nice her laugh was.

"I would not be cute like you if I put my hood up

like that." He chuckled. "I would look like some teenager trying to be cool."

"Oh, I don't know, I think you might look cute. Or maybe you would look cool—like you were on a secret mission."

"That's me, the James Bond of Rosewood Beach."

She laughed again, and he realized that he was moving the magnet back and forth again, even faster this time.

"I wish I could ask you to swoop in and save the day, James Bond of Rosewood Beach." She sighed.

His heart twisted as he thought to himself that he wished he could swoop in and help her with her troubles. "I'm sure you don't need me. You're brilliant. You'll come up with a way to help your family."

"That's sweet of you to say. I'm trying. I keep thinking about it, and I'm sure I'll come up with something. Eventually."

"Well, you're not alone. You've got a whole town here to support you—" *and me*, he thought privately —"and I know your siblings will be a huge help to you as well. Your family seems really tight-knit. I'm sure you're all going to do everything you can to help, using all your different strengths."

There was a short pause, and then she said, "Thank you, Cooper." She sounded touched. Then she gasped. "Oh! Yes! Thank you, seriously, thank you, you just gave me a great idea. My siblings and I need to pull together and use our different abilities to help! You're brilliant."

"I am?" He couldn't help grinning, hearing her sound so excited, but he wasn't sure how he had helped. He wanted her to explain her idea, but—

"I'll talk to you again soon. I should go. I'm really excited about this."

"Okay—"

"Thank you again!"

"Wait a second—do you want to go bowling Wednesday night?" He blurted out the words in a hurry, wanting to make sure he caught her before she hung up.

"I'd love to." She sounded as though she was smiling. "See you Wednesday."

"See you Wednesday. Bye."

She hung up, and he stared at his blank phone screen for a few moments, feeling his heart buzz with a kind of excitement that he hadn't felt in years.

"Pass me the potatoes, Dean. No, not the green beans, the potatoes!"

Julia chuckled quietly as she watched Hazel sigh

with exasperation over the way her twin wasn't paying attention to what she was saying. Dean had clearly been lost in thought, although he didn't seem particularly down.

All of her siblings had gathered for dinner at Vivian's house, and—despite the painful absence of their father—it almost felt like old times. Vivian had soft jazz music playing on the radio in the background, and the familiar dining room was filled with the mouthwatering aromas of mashed potatoes with gravy, green beans, cornbread muffins, and Chicken Marsala. The lights were warm and cozy, and through the windows of the dining room, they could see the sky beginning to turn pink from the sunset.

"Oops." Dean grinned at Hazel and passed her the potatoes. "Sorry."

"Penny for your thoughts," Julia teased him, helping herself to a cornbread muffin. "You seem like you're pretty deep in thought there."

"Oh, just thinking about the whole Judd McCormick debacle. Wouldn't it be nice if we could just prank him, like Hazel and I used to do when we were kids, and then he'd go away?"

"You mean like Mr. Sanders?" Vivian asked, the familiar maternal sternness in her voice.

Dean threw back his head laughing. "You remembered!"

"How could I forget my children covering the car of one of our neighbors with plastic spiders?" Vivian said, still frowning, although she seemed to be trying to repress a smile.

"He was so mean." Hazel laughed, shaking her head. "He was always yelling at us."

"And then he moved away, right after the spider incident." Dean grinned triumphantly.

"He moved away to be with his sister in Florida," Vivian said, shaking her head and laughing.

"And because of the plastic spiders, I'm convinced." Hazel tapped her chin. "Do we still have those somewhere?"

Julia shook her head, amused by her siblings. She made eye contact across the table with Alexis, who was laughing quietly into her glass of sparkling water.

"I don't think pranks are going to fix the Judd McCormick problem," Julia said. "But something needs to be done, for everyone's sakes. It's clear that any kind of brewery wouldn't be as popular as the pub is, even if they make it a kind of restaurant." Julia shook her head. "It's like he thinks our location is all he needs, but he wouldn't have our recipes or our cooks or anything that makes The Lighthouse Grill feel homey to all our regulars."

"The brewery is all stark and modern," Hazel said. "Not at all attractive. I bet Judd would try to make his new building look like that too."

"That wouldn't suit the people here," Vivian agreed, looking thoughtful. "People in Rosewood Beach like comfort. It's such a beautiful town—some ugly modern building is hardly going to attract people's respect."

"So we need to fight to stay," Julia said, looking around at all of her siblings. "We don't want Rosewood Beach to lose its favorite restaurant to something that isn't going to be as popular. Judd thinks he's got it all figured out, but the sale would end up being a bad thing for him too, I'm sure."

"How do you know all this?" Dean asked, looking confused.

"Uh, we might have spied a little." Hazel grinned.

"What?" Vivian asked, sounding alarmed, and Julia and Hazel were quick to reassure her.

"We didn't do anything we shouldn't have." Julia chuckled, remembering their hoods. Her stomach glowed with happiness when she thought of Cooper calling her "cute" during their phone call earlier that night.

"We just went to the McCormick brewery and went on part of a tour. We meant to go on the whole thing, but then Judd started looking at us like he recognized us." Hazel wrinkled her nose. "We put our hoods up so we—"

"You put your hoods up?" Dean threw his head back, crowing with laughter. "Hey, look at us, we're not conspicuous at all!"

Hazel balled up her napkin and threw it at him. He dodged it calmly, still laughing. Vivian and Julia were laughing, too, and even Alexis was starting to giggle.

"We did look pretty silly." Julia grinned. "But I think it worked—for the most part."

"You're full-fledged spies now." Alexis wiped a tear away, shaking with laughter. "Will you be offering your services for hire?"

"Oh, for sure." Hazel grinned. "Next time I'll even wear a color other than bright blue."

Everyone around the table continued to laugh. Although the situation was funny, their laughter had an almost wild quality to it, as if their emotions were ready to indulge in a release from sorrow. Julia smiled to herself, glad that her and Hazel's escapade had served to lighten the atmosphere.

"So we need to save the pub," Hazel said, bringing the conversation back to where it needed to be.

"We need to do everything we can," Julia agreed. "And I thought of something that should be able to help us, earlier." She paused, wondering how exactly she should phrase her idea.

"What?" Dean prompted, leaning forward. He looked excited, and she smiled at him, feeling a rush of affection for his energetic spirit.

"We need a loan in order to make up for the money that Dad lost in gambling." Julia spoke slowly, choosing her words carefully. "Alexis, would Grayson consider giving us a loan?"

Everyone turned to Alexis, whose face had gone white. Julia's lips parted, wondering why her sister suddenly looked ashen when she had been laughing only a few moments before.

The table went silent, and everyone stared at Alexis in concern.

"I—I don't think so," Alexis stammered, her voice breaking a little.

"Why not?" Hazel asked, sounding shocked. "I mean, he's your husband, and he's loaded, so—"

Vivian shook her head at Hazel, warning her to hush. It was clear that something was wrong, since a large tear was rolling down Alexis's cheek.

"Alexis," Julia asked softly. "Is something else the matter?"

"Yes," Alexis blurted, starting to cry. "My relationship with Grayson is on the rocks. I don't know how it started or how to fix it, but he barely speaks to me anymore, and he—I—I can't ask him for anything." She let out a sob and stood up hurriedly. "Excuse me," she said and ran out of the room.

Hazel pressed her hand against her mouth, and Dean stared at Alexis's exit with his jaw dropped.

"Oh, my poor girl," murmured Vivian. "That's awful. No wonder she's been so quiet this whole time. I got the impression that something else was grieving her, but I kept telling myself it was just your father's passing."

"That's too much for anyone to be dealing with at once." Julia shook her head, feeling a surge of sympathy for her sister. "I had no idea she was going through that."

"I should have guessed." Hazel sighed. "She was crying the other morning, and I think she was about to tell me about Grayson, but then she didn't."

"She probably feels ashamed," Julia said softly,

thinking of how reluctant she'd been to share the news that she'd been fired.

"I feel terrible for her," Dean said, shaking his head. "Grayson never seemed like a total fool to me, but I guess he is if he's letting his relationship with Alexis go like that."

"I'm going to go get her a cookie or something," Hazel said, standing up. "Mom, do you have any—"

"Yes, in the cookie jar." Vivian smiled fondly at her daughter, although her eyes still looked troubled.

"I'll come too." Dean stood up.

"No, we can't all go." Hazel shook her head. "You guys finish your dinner. I just want to check on her."

"Okay." Dean sighed and sat down again. "But bring her a glass of milk too. You know she likes to dunk her cookies."

Hazel grinned at him and disappeared. For a moment, everyone remaining at the table was silent.

"When she comes back, we'll remind her that she'll always have us," Vivian said softly. "We'll help her get through this."

Julia nodded, feeling sorry for her sister and wondering what they would do without Grayson's support. She took a deep breath, knowing that no matter what happened, they were going to figure something out and not give up.

CHAPTER SEVENTEEN

Vivian drove up to Hazel's cottage and parked her car carefully. Early morning sunlight sparkled on the windows of the house and gleamed on the colored glass garden ornaments that dotted the front garden. Vivian had always felt proud of Hazel for creating such a wonderful home for herself and Samantha. Every time she'd visited her daughter, she'd felt as though she was going to a place that was going to bring her comfort and happiness.

Today she didn't feel the same way, but that was no fault of Hazel's. The night before, Alexis hadn't returned to the dinner table, and she and Hazel had left shortly after everyone else had finished eating. Vivian's heart ached for her daughter, and she was there at Hazel's house hoping that she could talk to Alexis and help her feel better about her situation with Grayson.

She got out of her car and walked slowly up the path to the front door, which was painted a cheerful mint green. She knocked softly, and a moment later the door was opened by Hazel, who was still wearing her pajamas with an apron tied on over them.

"Hey, sweetheart." Vivian gave Hazel a hug. "How are you this morning?"

"Oh, I'm okay." Hazel smiled at her mother as they pulled away from the hug, but then she sighed. "Alexis was quiet all the way home last night. I've been up for over an hour already, and I haven't seen her yet this morning."

"I feel so bad for her." Vivian followed Hazel as they walked slowly toward Hazel's kitchen. The air was filled with the warm, buttery aroma of waffles and the nutty fragrance of coffee. "I didn't realize that Alexis was having so much trouble. I feel as though I should have realized it, somehow. I think I might have if I wasn't so bogged down with my own grief."

Hazel shook her head. "You couldn't have known, Mom. It's clear she didn't want to tell anyone about it, so she must have been trying to keep it from us. All we can expect when someone's going through something so sensitive like that is that they'll confide in us when they're ready. She wasn't ready until last night." Hazel bustled around in her kitchen as she spoke, getting a cup of coffee ready for her mother.

"You're right." Vivian sighed, and then gratefully accepted the cup of coffee that her daughter handed to her. "But I don't think she was even ready to tell us last night. We kind of forced it out of her by accident."

"True. But I think it'll be better for her now that it's out in the open." Hazel went back to the stove, where she was making waffles. "Now we can support her, since we know what's going on. Before, she didn't have anyone she could talk to about this. That must have been awful."

For a few more minutes, Hazel and Vivian worked quietly in the kitchen together. Vivian helped set the table for breakfast while Hazel finished making the waffles and cut up fresh strawberries into thin slices. Vivian was lost in thought as they worked. She wanted to make Alexis feel better, and she kept wondering what she could do to lift her daughter's spirits.

"Good morning!"

Samantha sashayed into the kitchen, followed by Alexis. They were both smiling, and Vivian's heart lifted with relief when she saw that her daughter was feeling better.

"Good morning." Hazel gave Samantha a hug, and then gave Alexis one as well. "How are you both feeling?"

"Great." Samantha slid into a chair at the kitchen table. "Wow, these waffles smell amazing."

"I feel better." Alexis gave Vivian and Hazel a watery smile. "Samantha cheered me up."

Hazel gave her daughter a high-five. "That's my girl. Way to go. You're a sweetheart to help your aunt out like that."

Samantha smiled, looking happy. Then she noticed the time on the clock hanging on the wall behind her mother's shoulder and gasped. "Oh, shoot! I overslept. The bus is going to be here in a couple of minutes."

Hazel sprang into action. "Take a waffle," she said, sliding one into a Ziploc bag. "I'll save you a couple so you can have them with the strawberries and whipped cream when you come home."

"Amazing, thanks, Mom!" Samantha grabbed the

Ziploc bag, threw her backpack on over her shoulder, and hurried out the back door. "Bye, everybody!"

"Bye!" they all called, even though the door had swung shut behind her already.

"That girl is a treasure," Hazel said fondly, bringing the bowl of freshly cut strawberries over to the kitchen table. "Come on, you two, let's eat these waffles while they're hot. There's nothing better than waffles with strawberries and whipped cream for breakfast, if I do say so myself."

Vivian smiled at her daughter, thinking to herself that Hazel was a treasure as well. If she remembered correctly, Hazel's favorite breakfast food was a skillet with plenty of bacon, potatoes, and cheese, and waffles with strawberries and whipped cream was Alexis's favorite breakfast food.

The three of them sat down at the table together, and for a few minutes, they ate in comfortable silence. The waffles were deliciously light and fluffy, and the strawberries added a pleasantly tangy flavor to the sweetness of the whipped cream.

"I know you're both trying to cheer me up," Alexis said finally, looking up from her food and smiling at her mother and sister. "I appreciate it, I really do."

Vivian   reached   over   and   squeezed   her

daughter's hand. "Whenever you feel ready to tell us about it, we're here to listen. We love you so much, Alexis."

"Thanks, Mom." Alexis blinked back a few tears. "I love you both so much too. I don't know what I'd do if I had to face this without my family."

"Well, you don't have to." Hazel gave her a reassuring smile. "We're here for you."

Alexis smiled back at her, and then let out a long sigh. "I would like to talk about it, but I hardly know where to begin."

"When did you first feel that your relationship was getting rocky?" Vivian asked gently.

"Oh, it all seemed to happen gradually. At first, I convinced myself that it would just be a temporary thing. He'd get so busy with work and brush off our date nights. At first, he tried to reschedule them, but then he stopped doing that. We—we've just been drifting apart. He doesn't have time for me anymore, and he doesn't make time. We don't talk like we used to, and no matter what I've tried or said, it hasn't gotten better. I—I think I'm losing him." Her voice cracked on her last words, and she covered her face with her hands.

Hazel and Vivian exchanged a troubled glance. As much as she hated the idea, Vivian had to admit to herself that it looked as though Alexis's marriage with Grayson was coming to an end.

"It's all going to be okay." Hazel stood up and walked around the table to her sister. She gave her a hug. "I remember feeling like how you do now when Simon and I decided to get a divorce. At the time, I felt like my world was ending and I didn't think I'd ever really be happy again. But I was so wrong. There's life after heartbreak. There really is."

Alexis hiccupped, nodding. "Thank you. I know you're right, but I—well, it still doesn't feel that way."

"I know." Hazel sighed as she returned to her chair. "You'll just have to give it time. But when it feels hard, remind yourself that you're going to feel so much joy again."

Vivian felt tears rise to her eyes as she reflected that Hazel's advice was good for her to hear as well.

"I also want to apologize for how we handled last night," Hazel said. "Julia and I, I mean. We got carried away, trying to come up with a plan, and I'm sorry if we seemed insensitive."

Alexis shook her head. "You couldn't have known. I tried to keep it a secret. I—I didn't want to tell anyone. I was hoping I would never have to. I was hoping that Grayson would start to fight for our marriage and that no one would ever know we'd been struggling. But I have to face the music, and the reality is that we're slipping further and further away from each other."

Alexis stared down at her plate for a few heartbeats, and a tear rolled down her cheek. Hazel and Vivian exchanged another worried look.

"Things will be all right," Vivian said, wishing with all her might that she could somehow just snap her fingers and make everything okay again for her daughter. "You have us. We're going to support you through this."

"And it isn't over yet." Hazel's blue-green eyes were full of empathy as she looked at her sister. "Stay positive for as long as you can. Things may still get better between you and Grayson."

Alexis nodded, smiling weakly. "Thank you both. I feel a bit better—well, better supported at least." Her smile widened and she looked almost happy.

"Good. Whenever you're feeling down, just know that you can talk to us." Hazel reached across the table and squeezed her sister's hand. "And try to keep your mind off it as much as you can. I'll do my best to distract you. You want some more waffles?"

"Yes, please." Alexis laughed. "These are wonderful."

All three of them had second helpings of the waffles, and Vivian felt a rush of happiness as she watched her daughters smile and talk to each other. She felt very proud of her family, and grateful that she had them by her side.

.

CHAPTER EIGHTEEN

Cooper paced back and forth in the living room, checking his watch every few seconds. The babysitter who he'd hired to babysit Macey during his date with Julia wasn't late yet, but she only had a couple more minutes until she was, and he didn't see any new cars outside his house. If she was late, it would make him even more nervous than he already was, since it would be a sign of irresponsibility.

The babysitter was a local teenager who'd come highly recommended by some people at work. He'd been told that she was kind, responsible, and great with kids, but he still felt fluttery with anxiety. He didn't like the idea of leaving Macey with a stranger, even when it was a stranger he'd been assured he could trust.

In the next moment, he saw a car drive up to the house and park along the curb. He let out a sigh of relief. He wanted plenty of time to make sure Macey would be okay with being alone with the young woman, and he also didn't want to be late for his date with Julia.

"Hey, Macey!" he called. "Your new friend is here!"

Macey looked up from where she was playing on the living room couch. She frowned a little, as if doubtful that the person who was arriving was anything to celebrate.

The teenager walked up to the front door, smiling and looking cheerful. She had braces and a ponytail, and her eyes were kind. Cooper felt relieved when he saw her crouch down and introduce herself to Macey without any kind of hesitation, and Macey even offered the babysitter a small smile.

He stayed for another ten minutes or so, making sure that Macey wasn't feeling too anxious, and making sure that Callie, the babysitter, knew where everything was located and what his phone number was.

"Okay." He sighed as he looked at his watch, realizing that he needed to leave in another few minutes if he was going to be on time. "You call me if you have any questions, Callie. Anything at all."

"You enjoy your date, Mr. Harris." Callie grinned at him from where she was sitting with Macey on the rug. "Macey and I are going to watch a movie, aren't we, Macey?"

Macey looked up and seemed to realize that Cooper was leaving. Her bottom lip started to tremble and she stood up and ran over to him. His heart melted and he gave her a big hug.

"I'm going to be back really soon," he said. "I'll only be gone a few hours."

"Hours?" Macey's voice rose in pitch, as if she considered hours to be the equivalent of weeks.

"Hours go by really fast, Macey, especially when you're having as much fun as we'll be having," Callie said, coming over to the little girl. Cooper felt reassured by how calm the teenager was acting in spite of Macey's tears. "We're going to have so much fun. I'm so excited. Are you excited?"

Macey frowned doubtfully, but she stopped crying. Cooper bent down and kissed her head.

"I'm going to see our friend Julia, honey. Should I say hi for you?"

Macey nodded, and he waved to her as he said goodbye and slipped out the door. He did it quickly, hoping she wouldn't start crying again before he could leave. He didn't think he'd be able to go if she was crying as he left.

He took a deep breath as he made his way to the garage. He glanced back at the house, still feeling nervous about the whole thing.

This Callie seems like a great babysitter, he reassured himself. *And besides—what would you tell Julia if you decided to cancel?*

Julia. At the thought of her, he had a different kind of jitters. He smiled, suddenly feeling buoyant, and hurried into the garage.

He arrived at Julia's mother's house a few minutes later. He parked on the street outside the house, and then hurried up the front path to the door. He was a minute late, and he felt badly about it. He had a feeling that Julia was the kind of person who was always early to everything.

He rang the doorbell and waited. Around him, the wind sighed in the branches of the trees, and the last traces of the sunset glowed along the eastern edge of the sky. Julia opened the door a moment later, and his breath caught when he saw her.

She was wearing casual clothes, jeans and a baggy sweater, and her face was shining with excitement.

"Hey." She grinned at him, and he grinned back at her.

"Hey. You—you look really nice."

She laughed and looked down at her clothes. "I haven't dressed like this in years. I don't normally do fun and casual things like this. You're making me feel like I'm in some old-time movie, getting picked up by my date for a night on the town."

He laughed. He liked hearing himself described at her date. "Well, I hope we have an evening worthy of the silver screen. May I offer you my arm?"

She laughed and linked her arm through his as they walked down the front path to his car. His heart felt warm and buoyant, and he realized that he was falling for her more and more.

It was a short drive to the bowling alley. They bought a pizza and some soft drinks at the food counter, and then went to get the equipment they needed. He chose a plain black bowling ball, and she chose a sparkling purple one.

"I'm pretty sure I used this one in high school," she said, laughing as they returned to their spot, wearing their bowling shoes and carrying their bowling balls. "No matter how old I get, I can't resist that feminine urge to hold something sparkly."

He laughed, and they started their game

together. She was competitive in a fun way, always assuring him she was going to beat him. They were both fairly good bowlers, so it was a close game, which made it even more enjoyable. They played slowly, eating their pizza and taking sips of their drinks as they played.

Julia won their first game, and the gleeful dance of victory she did made Cooper almost double over with laughter. He hadn't expected her to be someone with such a fun side to her.

"So," she said, sitting down at the table and picking up another slice of pizza. "Tell me about yourself, Cooper Harris. Where did you learn to be actually decent bowling competition for me?"

He chuckled and sat down across from her, taking another slice as well. "I don't know—I guess I've gone bowling a fair amount in my life. It was something my friends and I used to do in high school too."

She nodded, munching on her pizza and smiling at him. "What were you like in high school?"

He shook his head. "I have no idea. The same, but skinnier?" He laughed.

She laughed too. "No, I mean, like—what were your interests? Like, what was your favorite band?"

He didn't have to think about it, he knew the

answer right away. "The Barn Rollers. I listened to them all the time. I still do."

She stared at him for a couple of seconds, and then she let out a giggle.

"What?" he protested, starting to laugh too. "They're a great band."

"Sure, if you like that kind of music."

"You don't like country music?"

"Do I look like I live in Texas?"

He shook his head, laughing harder. "Oh, come on. I love country music. It's got soul and emotion and it talks about real people living good lives. What other music genre does that as well?"

She shrugged. "I guess you've got a point there. I don't listen to country music, so I couldn't tell you how good for the soul it is."

"Oh, we'll have to change that at some point. I'll have to get you to like it."

"Mmm." She shook her head dubiously, laughing.

"Just wait until you see a live country music concert. Concerts are the best way to experience music, I think. There's so much sound and excitement everywhere. All the people around you are singing along, and... it's like the full experience."

She was gazing at him with warmth in her eyes,

and he felt as though the tips of his ears were turning slightly pink.

"Was going to see The Barn Rollers your favorite concert?" she asked, smiling at him.

He shook his head. "Actually, I've never seen them in concert. I've always wanted to. It's on my bucket list for sure."

They started another game, and this time it was even closer. He was still enjoying himself immensely, but he found himself starting to worry about Macey. He hadn't gotten any calls or texts from Callie, but rather than reassure him, that made him nervous. He wished he'd asked the teenager to regularly send him updates, letting him know how everything was going. He hated the idea of Macey being at home and sad without him.

"Cooper?"

He turned to Julia and saw that she was smiling at him.

"What?" he asked, realizing that she'd said something to him and he'd been so lost in thought that he didn't hear her.

"It's your turn." She hesitated, watching his face for a moment. "Is everything all right? You were looking kind of worried."

He smiled, admiring how perceptive she was. "I

am a little bit. Nothing's wrong, but Macey's at home with a new babysitter, and I was just wishing I was getting more updates. I'm sure she's okay, but—well, she started crying when I was leaving and I'm worried that she's still upset."

Julia nodded, looking sympathetic. "How did the babysitter handle her crying?"

"Oh, just great. She seemed totally calm and got her to stop. And I think she'd call me if Macey was really upset, but—oh, I don't know." He sighed. "I'm just jittery about it."

"I understand." She touched his arm, and he smiled at her.

"The babysitter came highly recommended, so I shouldn't worry. She's a teenager, but I guess she's been babysitting for years."

"Is it Callie Rogers by any chance?"

"Yes! Do you know her?"

"I do." Julia grinned at him. "My sister Hazel used to hire her to babysit my niece Samantha. She's a real pro. She's been babysitting since she was twelve. Hazel always said she was the best babysitter in Rosewood Beach."

His face brightened into a smile when he heard Julia's words. "Well, at least I picked the best babysitter in town." He laughed. "But the truth is, no matter how good at her job Callie is, I still feel bad about leaving Macey there without me. She's so little to be placed with a total stranger all night. I wonder if I'm doing right by her."

Julia nodded. "Let's take another food break and talk about it." She smiled sweetly at him. "That thin-crust pizza left me feeling hungry. You want to get some hot dogs and French fries?"

He grinned at her. "Sounds great to me."

They went back up to the food window and ordered two hot dogs and a small basket of fries to split.

"Just ketchup, huh?" he teased her as she drew a thin, straight line of ketchup on her hot dog. They were standing at the edge of the food counter, which had been stocked with numerous condiments.

She laughed. "I like a neat hot dog. I'm not a wild person, like you over there."

He chuckled, looking down at the mess of relish, mustard, and ketchup that was covering his hot dog. "You'll have to take a bite out of mine. You don't know what you're missing."

"Mm, I better grab some extra napkins."

Laughing, they returned to their table and sat down. Julia took a long sip of her unfinished soft drink and then smiled at Cooper. "So. Tell me more about how you're feeling."

His eyebrows lifted as he wondered for a moment if she was talking about how he was feeling about their date, and her.

She seemed to guess his thoughts, because her eyebrows rose as well and she hurriedly added, "About leaving Macey with the babysitter tonight."

"Oh." He smiled, feeling his jitters disappear but also feeling slightly disappointed. He realized that he wanted to talk with her about how he was feeling about her. "Well, it's hard being a single father. I have to work, but that means putting Macey in daycare a great deal of the time. She loves her teachers and her friends at daycare, but I always feel a little guilty about not being there for her. And tonight's the first time I've left her alone with someone she didn't know."

Julia nodded, listening intently as he spoke. "Your circumstances are hard. And they're not ideal for Macey, but that's not your fault. You're clearly doing your best, and I know she knows how much you love her. And as far as tonight goes, I know she's old enough to understand that you're coming back. I bet she's having an amazing time with Callie right now, playing some game and giggling."

He smiled at her, feeling a warm glow In his chest. Not only was the scene that Julia had just described to him reassuring, but he felt grateful for the way she was making sure he felt better about his situation. It had been a long time since he'd had someone in his life who he could really talk to about how he was feeling, and he felt as though some of the weight had lifted from his shoulders.

"Thanks, Julia. I appreciate you saying all that."

She nodded. "All you can do is your best. This isn't really a worthy comparison, but with my job back in New York, I did everything I thought was right and I still made a mistake that cost me my job. At the time, it felt like I hadn't done enough and what happened was my fault. But the truth was, I did my best, and that's all anyone can do. My job ending brought me here—it's what allows me to stay here in Rosewood Beach for a while. The world didn't end. Sometimes it feels like the circumstances are stacked against us, and our best isn't enough, but it is. Things will always work out in the end, as long as you keep doing what you can. Don't be hard on yourself for doing your best."

"Thank you." His heart was beating faster as he looked into her kind eyes. He felt himself becoming more and more attracted to this insightful, thoughtful woman. "Would it be all right if I kissed you?"

Julia flushed slightly. "Yes." She looked up at him with shining eyes.

The world seemed to stop for a few moments as he leaned toward her and kissed her mouth gently.

He would have kissed her longer, but in the next moment, a group of nearby kids let out a shout of victory, startling him and Julia out of their kiss.

She turned toward the teenagers, laughing. "Looks like somebody got a strike."

The kids continued to laugh and talk loudly in celebration, and Cooper chuckled.

"I guess I should have picked a more romantic spot than a bowling alley."

She shook her head. "This is perfect. Besides," she added a touch shyly, "since I'll be in Rosewood Beach for a little while, at least, there's plenty of time for us to find more romantic places to go on dates to."

His heart lifted up at her words, and he nodded in agreement. "That sounds great. Meanwhile, how about you have this last bite of my hot dog? I promise you're going to... well, I promise you won't hate it."

"I accept your offer." Grinning, Julia ate the last bite of his hot dog. She wiped smears of relish and mustard off her fingers as she chewed, scrunching up her nose a little. Then she nodded and swallowed. "Okay. You're right. That's really good."

"For the win!" He laughed.

"Speaking of winning, it's time for me to beat you in bowling again. What do you say we go back to our game?"

They spent the rest of the night talking and laughing as they bowled. By the time he dropped her off at Vivian's house, he felt as though he was going to be counting the hours until he could see her again.

CHAPTER NINETEEN

Julia took a deep breath of the fragrant spring air as she walked along the sidewalk. It was late in the morning on the day after her date with Cooper, and she'd gotten up with the sun, feeling wide-awake and full of energy from the moment her eyes opened.

Last night was amazing, she thought, thinking of their kiss and smiling uncontrollably. *I feel attracted to him in a way I've never felt with anyone before. He's so thoughtful, and fun, and...*

She pressed her lips together, getting a rush of nervousness as she remembered how complicated their situation was. Then she brushed those thoughts aside. She was starting to fall hard enough that she could tell herself that things could work out between her and Cooper. She didn't know yet what the logistics would be, but she liked him enough to be willing to make compromises.

She sighed dreamily as she tucked her manicured hands inside the pockets of her raincoat. She glanced down at the faint white paint stain that was still on her sleeve from when Cooper had caught in her in the rain, and she smiled. Now that paint stain was her favorite thing about the coat, she thought cheerfully.

She turned a corner and saw Alexis sitting on a bench up ahead. She waved her hand in greeting, but Alexis, who was wearing sunglasses and staring straight ahead, didn't seem to notice her. Julia's heart twisted with concern for her sister and she hurried along the sidewalk toward her.

"Hey," she said as she reached Alexis's side. "Sorry if I'm a little late. I thought we said ten-fifteen."

Alexis gave her a faint smile and took off her sunglasses. "No, you're right. I'm just here early. I—I couldn't sleep well last night, so I got up early."

Julia swallowed, feeling bad for Alexis. While she herself had been up early with excitement about a potential new relationship, her sister had been up all night worrying about her relationship falling apart.

"I'm sorry to hear that." She sat down next to Alexis and gave her a hug. "Hopefully our shopping trip this morning helps boost your spirits."

She and Alexis had arranged to meet up and shop for makeup at a local boutique. They were the two "city girls" of the Owens family, and they loved getting to shop together because they shared the same appreciation for fashion trends in makeup and clothing.

Alexis smiled weakly. "Ordinarily, retail therapy wouldn't be able to do much for me in this state, but getting to shop with you is a whole other matter."

"That's the spirit!" Julia squeezed her sister's hand. "I think they have our favorite brands here. I've been dying to get that new eye shadow palate I showed you the other day."

"Should we go in?" Alexis still seemed tired and listless, but her smile broadened a little at the mention of the eye shadow palate. She had been excited about the colors when Julia had showed it to her on her phone the other night.

"Yes please. It's that store on the corner, right?"

"Yes." Alexis stood. "That little pink one."

"It's so charming. Sometimes I really miss Rosewood Beach. It's like everywhere I turn here, I see something beautiful."

"I know what you mean." Alexis sighed. "L.A. has some really beautiful spots, but it's not the same as home."

For a moment, the two sisters shared a smile, and then they strolled down the sidewalk and stepped inside the boutique together. The store was cool and smelled fragrantly of lavender and cedar. Soft jazz music was playing on hidden speakers. A cheerfully smiling woman standing behind the front counter greeted them.

"Can I help you find anything today?" she asked. She was wearing a smart pink blazer, and Julia admired the way she'd done her hair in a smooth French twist.

"We're just browsing for now, but I'll let you know if we have any questions." Julia smiled at her.

The sisters began to wander through the store together, but Julia found herself looking more at Alexis than at the makeup products. She could tell that Alexis was fighting back tears as they went, and none of the products seemed to be catching her interest at all. Alexis was usually cooing and chattering with excitement whenever she and Julia went makeup shopping together, and Julia felt her stomach twist with concern.

As they stopped in front of the lipstick section,

Julia put on her brightest smile, hoping to cheer her sister up.

"I think one of these pink shades would look darling on you. What about this one? Dusty rose?"

Alexis looked down at the lipsticks and tears started to well up in her eyes.

"Oh, honey," Julia said. "Picking a lipstick shade is no cause for tears."

She'd hoped her gentle teasing might lift her sister's spirits, but instead, Alexis took a shaky breath and a couple of the tears spilled out of her eyes.

"Can we just make our purchases and leave?" Alexis whispered, barely able to get the words out.

"Sure." Julia laid a reassuring hand on her sister's shoulder for a moment. "We definitely can."

She quickly picked out a lipstick shade for herself—a color that she already knew she liked—and they went up to the counter to pay for their makeup. The store owner seemed cheerfully unaware of how close to tears Alexis was, which Julia felt was a blessing.

As they stepped back out into the fresh spring air, Julia glanced down the street and noticed the windows of Ocean Breeze Café gleaming pleasantly in the sunlight.

"How about we go to Ocean Breeze Café for

lunch?" she suggested. "I didn't eat breakfast, and my stomach is really starting to growl."

"I didn't either," Alexis admitted, her voice still hushed from trying not to cry.

"Well, there you go! Not eating will always make things seem worse than they are. Food is an important way of bolstering the spirits." She smiled at Alexis, but her sister was just staring straight ahead and seemed to have not heard her.

They made their way to Ocean Breeze Café and got a charming little table by the window. After they'd both ordered eggs benedict and hot chocolates, Alexis seemed steadier emotionally. She took a deep breath and looked Julia in the eyes.

"Okay. I know I should tell you what's been happening. It feels better to not have all this be a secret anymore, and I—well, I think I should talk about this new development with someone."

Julia nodded, her heart thumping with concern. She wondered what the new development was.

"I was making a payment to my and Grayson's joint account," Alexis said, her voice soft. She stared down at the table in front of them. "I saw a charge to this high-end downtown restaurant in L.A. It's pricey there, but the bill still looked like a dinner for two. I—I'm worried that all of this—him not returning my calls, his lack of effort in our relationship—means that he's been busy with another woman."

Julia's heart gave a jolt. "Oh, no—Alexis—there's no way that could be true. Grayson is just busy with work, he's not that kind of guy."

"Well, Mom didn't think Dad was a gambler either," Alexis said, looking up from the table. Her eyes were brimming with tears again.

"Julia and Alexis Owens!" A woman wearing a bright purple sweater hurried up to their table, all smiles. "So good to see you both."

"Hi, Alice," Julia said, smiling at the woman as she remembered her. "Good to see you too."

"Would you pass along a compliment to your mother and the chefs at The Lighthouse Grill? I just loved their latest dinner special, and so did my elderly father-in-law. He hasn't been able to talk about anything else. He keeps asking when they're going to have it again." She laughed a loud laugh that reminded Julia of bells tinkling.

"I'm so glad." Julia smiled at her. "I'll be sure to pass the compliment along."

"Well, I won't keep you. Have a great day, both of you!"

"You as well!"

Julia waved goodbye to Alice, and Alexis mustered a smile of farewell as the other woman stepped out of the cafe. Julia turned back to her sister with a frown of worry, her mind back on what Alexis had told her before Alice had come to speak with them.

"Don't stress about it. You know he goes out to eat with other businessmen all the time. He probably just paid someone's tab as a way of earning favor."

Alexis pressed her lips together, looking doubtful, and at that moment, their waitress returned to their table with the hot chocolates.

"Your food should be out in a couple of minutes," she said. "And I overheard just now that you're the Owens sisters. I'd thought so, but I wasn't sure. I want to offer my condolences about your father."

"Thank you." Julia felt touched by the woman's kind manner.

"How is Vivian doing?" the waitress asked. "Is The Lighthouse Grill going to be all right?"

Julia sighed. "I hope so. We're doing everything we can."

The waitress nodded, and then lowered her voice. "That man—that Judd McCormick—has been lingering around more than ever. I know he's got all those fancy ideas about him and his sons taking over your property. I heard him talking about it on the phone to someone one day. I hope he won't manage it, but I know it's hard for small businesses to fight against these big ones that are expanding."

"I know." Julia nodded, doing her best to smile, but internally her heart was sinking. The waitress was right. They didn't stand much of a chance against the McCormicks.

"It would be such a shame if your pub turned into some silly brewery." The waitress sighed. "Rosewood Beach loves that place. It's been the town's favorite restaurant for years."

"Thank—oh!" Julia suddenly sat up straighter as she was struck with an idea.

"What?" Alexis asked, leaning forward.

"That's true. Our community loves the pub. What if we had a fundraiser for it? Save The Lighthouse Grill!"

"Oh, that sounds like a wonderful idea," said the waitress.

Alexis nodded, looking excited. "I think that could work," she said. Her sadness over Grayson seemed to be fading as she became enthusiastic about Julia's inspiration. "That's a great idea."

"We'll absolutely put up fliers here if you decide

to do that," the waitress assured them warmly. "Keep us posted."

She excused herself and returned a moment later with piping hot plates of eggs benedict. As she and Alexis started to eat the delicious food, Julia could see a worried frown return to her sister's face.

"Hey." She reached across the table and squeezed Alexis's hand. "Things are going to be okay with Grayson."

Alexis pressed her lips together. "I just—I'm not sure. I don't know what's going to happen."

"I understand. I can relate—since I'm jobless, I'm also in an uncertain place and I know how hard that is. But let's focus on what we do know—we're here together now, and we want to keep The Lighthouse Grill. Let's focus on saving the pub and push aside our other worries for a while."

Alexis nodded, smiling a little. "I agree. Let's focus on saving the pub."

They continued to eat their lunch, beginning to talk excitedly about what a fundraiser for The Lighthouse Grill could look like.

CHAPTER TWENTY

Cooper glanced up at Vivian's charming house as he walked up the front sidewalk. He felt butterflies dance in his chest, and he took a deep breath. He'd been to the house a couple of times to pick Julia up, but he'd never been inside it before. Now he was about to spend time with Julia and her family in the house.

She'd invited him to come over for dinner early that morning, and he'd accepted eagerly. He was looking forward to spending time with her, but he also felt nervous about going to dinner at her mother's house.

Still, I feel better than I did the other night, he thought to himself with a chuckle.

He'd hired Callie to babysit for him again, and it

was clear that she and Macey already had a bond. When he'd returned home from bowling with Julia the other night, Macey had been sound asleep and smiling happily. The next day, she'd kept talking excitedly about what a fun time she'd had with the babysitter.

He smiled to himself as he stepped up to the front door of the house. He was feeling better and more confident about everything—about his abilities as a single father, about leaving Macey with a babysitter, and about his blossoming relationship with Julia.

He rang the doorbell, feeling a surge of excitement overcome his flutters of nervousness. In the next second, Julia ripped the front door open and tugged him inside.

"Hi," she said breathlessly. "I need to talk to you."

"Oh, uh—" For a moment, he felt worried that something had gone wrong, but her eyes were bright and there was a smile on her face. "Sure."

Taking his hand, she led him into the living room. He got a quick glimpse of cream-colored walls covered in family photographs and a vase filled with fresh flowers on the mantelpiece before Julia practically pushed him onto the couch.

"Sit here. I have an idea." She stood in front of him, her cheeks flushed and her hands gesturing enthusiastically as she started to talk. "I think I know how we're going to save the pub. I had an idea when I was out with Alexis this morning, and now I've formed a plan. We're going to have a fundraiser to save the pub."

"Oh, that's a great idea!"

"Thank you. I'm still working out all of the details, but what I have so far is this. First, we advertise for the fundraiser in coffee shops, other restaurants, banks, and libraries. Also by word of mouth—that's huge here in Rosewood Beach. We'll need to spend some money on fliers, but not too much. I can cover those costs myself, as far as that goes."

He had to repress a smile, feeling charmed by the way she was describing her plan as if she was giving a presentation at a business meeting. Even though she was wearing jeans and a comfy sweater again, he could just picture her standing at the front of a long table in some work meeting, energetically outlining her ideas. She continued to speak, her eyes sparkling as she told him about everything she'd come up with.

"And the fundraiser itself will have to be planned out carefully. We want to make it a fun event that doesn't cost much to put on. We'll have plenty of games, a raffle, and a donation box, of course. I've already told a few people outside my family about the idea and everyone seems very excited about it. Our town loves The Lighthouse Grill, and I really think a fundraiser will give us the money we need to get things back in order and fill the holes—well, cover everything that's missing in our finances." Her cheeks flushed harder for a moment. "So, what do you think?"

His lips parted. She'd started to speak so quickly that he was still catching up to her, trying to process what she'd been saying. He hesitated, wanting to tell her how much he admired her but feeling as though that might be coming on too strong at that stage in their relationship.

Julia's expression fell, and she seemed to read his hesitation as a bad sign. "Sorry. I guess I seem pretty over the top to you."

He stood and took her in his arms. "Everyone should be over the top for their family." He smiled at her, and she grinned back at him. "What can I do to help?"

She lifted her face up to his and kissed him. "Thank you for being so wonderful." Her voice was a little breathless, and her eyes were starry. "If you would help with setting everything up, that would be most appreciated."

"You got it." He nodded, feeling a sense of excitement over both the plans for the fundraiser and their kiss.

"I can't wait to break the news to my mom!" Julia grinned, practically wiggling in his arms.

"Can't wait to break what news to me?" Vivian stepped through the doorway of the living room, looking excited.

"Mom! This is Cooper. Cooper, this is my mother."

"Very pleased to meet you, ma'am." He shook Vivian's hand, smiling at her.

"You as well. Julia's told me all kinds of great things about you, Cooper." Vivian's eyes were warm as she smiled back at him. "Dinner's all ready. Let's go eat and you can tell me about this news of yours."

"Cooper and I will tell you all about it during dinner, Mom," Julia said, linking arms with both her mother and Cooper. "You're going to be just as excited as we are."

CHAPTER TWENTY-ONE

Alexis couldn't help smiling as she gazed around her mother's living room. Her whole family was there, busily planning the fundraiser to save The Lighthouse Grill. There was a sense of excitement in the air that she found invigorating, and she felt grateful to have something to focus on other than her rocky marriage.

It was a beautiful, sunny Saturday morning, and the windows of the living room were open, letting in a fragrant breeze. Outside, birds chirped in the branches of the trees and the sound of someone singing in their backyard could be heard.

The Owens had worked together to make their planning meeting as enjoyable as possible. Dean had put on a playlist of soothing folk music, and

Hazel had brought a plate of chocolate chip peanut butter cookies for them to munch on as they worked. Each of them was planning the booth that they were going to run at the fundraiser, or planning out the details of a contribution they could make.

She looked down at the notes she'd been making and smiled. She'd volunteered to run a free "make-over" booth where she would do people's makeup and hair. She'd written up a list of all the supplies she would need, including a couple of mirrors, a comfortable chair, and plenty of beauty products. She felt excited about the prospect of making lots of people feel more beautiful and confident in themselves.

"What can I do at my booth?" Dean asked. He was leaning back in an armchair, staring at the ceiling. "I can't offer to fix people's cars from inside my booth at the pub."

"True, but you could teach them how to fix things themselves." Hazel smiled at her twin from where she was sitting on the rug in front of the coffee table. "And besides, you donating that car you restored for the auction is such a huge contribution already."

"Thanks, but I want to be part of the excitement

on the day of." Dean sighed and tapped his chin with his pencil.

"You'll think of something." Alexis smiled at him. "We'll all keep helping you brainstorm too."

The doorbell rang, and Julia hurried forward to get it.

"Who's that?" Hazel asked, cocking her head to one side in confusion. "Aren't we all here already?"

"We needed a second person to run the water games with you, Hazel." Julia's eyes were twinkling mischievously. "So I asked Jacob."

"Oh!" Hazel's cheeks flushed a bright pink. "Oh —um, okay."

Julia grinned and opened the front door. "Hey, Jacob! Come on in. Thanks so much for agreeing to this."

"Happy to help." Jacob stepped inside, smiling, and his eyes lighted on Hazel right away. He waved at her, and she waved back.

"I'll let Hazel explain our ideas to you," Julia said, looking impish. "I'm sure the two of you will come up with some great ideas together."

Jacob crossed the room to where Hazel was and sat down on the rug next to her without hesitation.

The work was fun, and it helped keep Alexis's

mind occupied. She'd been doing her best to not think about Grayson and her worries about her marriage, but occasionally thoughts of her husband snuck in despite her best efforts.

As she was sketching a plan of her booth, making sure that all of the products she wanted to have on hand would fit in her allotted space outside the pub, she started to think about her early days in L.A., when she worked part-time for a makeup company. She paused in her sketching, suddenly flooded with memories about her journey to L.A. and her modeling career, which at first had blossomed magnificently and then had steadily tampered off into an almost nonexistent hobby. She remembered the first night she'd met Grayson. He'd seemed so captivated by her, and she'd felt as though she was on top of the world.

Her stomach twisted as she remembered it. She tried to shake herself out of her reminiscing, telling herself to focus on the task at hand. The past was in the past, and there was no point in her thinking about it now.

She heard Hazel giggle, and she glanced over at Hazel and Jacob, who were laughing over something as they planned the water games together. Her heart ached as she watched them, recognizing the way her sister looked at Jacob. It was clear from her shining eyes that she had a major crush on him, and her smile made it clear that she was hopeful things might work out between them.

Alexis took a deep breath, trying not to feel jealous and out of sorts. She'd seen yet another charge on her and Grayson's joint credit card for an elegant restaurant, with a tab that was too expensive to have been for only one person. She had done her best to not think about it, but the uncertainty had been torturing her. She didn't know if she should bring it up with Grayson or not. Part of her felt strongly that she should voice her concerns to her husband, but the idea made her squirm with worry. She didn't know if Grayson would get upset with her for thinking something so despicable of him if it wasn't true—and if it was true, wouldn't he just lie to her anyway?

"Hey, Alexis, how's it going?"

She looked up, startled out of her reverie, and saw Julia standing beside her. Her sister reached over and gave her a hug, and Alexis wondered if Julia had sensed the way her spirits were crumbling.

"Good. I'm making sure that everything I want to

have on hand will fit in my booth." Alexis laughed breathlessly. Her heart felt as though it was beating faster than usual, and she wondered if she was flushed from worry.

"I know it will be amazing." Julia's voice was full of conviction. "I really think this is going to be the ticket to saving the pub and restoring Mom's strength. I think after this, she's going to know that she can go on in spite of Dad's lies and debts."

Alexis nodded. "I think you're right. I'm excited to see what this fundraiser does."

"And I think it will show our friend, Judd McCormick, and his sons, too, how much the people of this town love The Lighthouse Grill. Maybe they'll think twice about what they're trying to do after this."

Julia looked feisty as she spoke, and Alexis couldn't help smiling at her affectionately.

The doorbell rang, and everyone turned toward the door in surprise.

"Who is it this time?" Hazel asked, looking up.

"Pizza delivery?" Dean suggested hopefully.

Julia scampered over to the door and opened it.

"Cooper!" she cried eagerly and gave him a hug.

Cooper stood on the front step grinning, holding

the hand of his adorable little daughter and hugging Julia back with his free arm.

"I wanted to stop by with some good news." He stepped inside, followed by Macey, who looked around curiously and noticed the cookies on the coffee table with an exclamation of eagerness.

"We love good news!" Hazel grinned at him. "Come on in. And help yourselves to some cookies— I see Macey eyeing the plate." She laughed.

"Thanks, we will." He stepped over to the cookie plate and picked up a couple of cookies, handing one to Macey.

"Come on, spill the good news," Dean said. "Somebody bought my car already?"

Cooper laughed. "Not yet. But things are looking great. More items came in for the auction, and there's some pretty awesome stuff. And I added one myself —I'm offering to do a free landscaping of a backyard."

"Hey, that's awesome!"

"Great idea."

"Wow, thanks, Cooper."

Cooper grinned and Julia leaned over to him and kissed his cheek. "Thank you. That's huge. We really appreciate it."

"Yay!" Macey cried, clearly catching onto the

idea that something great was happening. Julia laughed and reached down to tickle the little girl's tummy, which made her giggle.

After a few minutes, Cooper went to talk to Dean, and Alexis turned to Julia with a smile. "You three all seem to be getting along well."

"We are." Julia glanced at Cooper with what could only be described as a starry-eyed smile. "He's such a great guy. He's working hard to be the best father he possibly can be, but it's like he doesn't know how great he is. He's so good about taking care of Macey. He really looks out for everyone—I mean, look at the way he's jumped into helping us with the fundraiser even though he's so busy."

Alexis nodded, smiling at her sister. "That is really sweet."

"I want to do something for him." Julia played with the end of her long, dark ponytail, twirling the strands between her fingers as she watched Cooper talk and laugh with Dean. "But I don't know what."

"You'll think of something." Alexis felt happy for her sister, but her heart still ached over Grayson.

But at least I have this fundraiser to focus on, she thought, trying to bolster her spirits. *It gives me something to do instead of just feel sorry for myself.*

She looked around the room, at her family and

friends talking and laughing excitedly about their plans, and she felt a faint glow of happiness fill her chest. She didn't know what was going to happen to her, but at least for the moment, she was there with people she loved.

CHAPTER TWENTY-TWO

Vivian leaned back in her desk chair and let out a long sigh. She stretched, feeling and hearing her back pop. She winced and glanced at the clock.

"Ten o'clock already," she muttered. "My goodness it's late."

She glanced out the window and smiled quietly to herself. She had a view of the ocean from her office at the pub, and for a few moments she watched the silver light of the moon dance on the tossing waves.

The pub had been closed for an hour already, since it was Sunday night and they didn't stay open late on Sundays. Most of the staff had gone home already, although she could still hear faint clinking sounds coming from the kitchen as it was being cleaned up. Once the pub had closed, she'd gone to her office to try to get a few additional things done for the upcoming fundraiser. She'd managed to stay focused despite her fatigue, and she'd accomplished everything she'd intended to, which was a good feeling.

Her eyes began to roam slowly around the room. It was filled with memories. She and Frank had hung up various awards and photographs on the walls over the years until they were nearly covered with frames. Moonlight glinted on the glass of the photographs, adding a dreamlike quality to their appearance.

Across from her desk was a large photograph of her and Frank standing outside the pub on the day it opened.

"Oh, Frank," she whispered, her eyes on the printed image of his face. "We were so full of dreams. We loved each other so much." She inhaled shakily. "Why didn't you tell me about your gambling?"

Sighing, she stood up and left the office, turning out the small lamp on the desk almost lovingly as she went. The hallway outside still smelled of salty, hearty food and she inhaled the comforting aroma, her mind on all of the things that had happened in the past few weeks.

She made her way to the dining room, which was empty of customers. The lights had been dimmed, and she found herself gazing around the room, filled with nostalgia. She had so many memories in that place—of some stressful days, certainly, and days of being exhausted, but for the most part her memories were full of joy. She'd worked there with her friends and her children and the man she loved. Most people, even rich people, weren't lucky enough to have a life like that.

She strolled slowly from table to table, thinking of all the thought and care she and Frank had put into designing and setting up their restaurant. "We built this place together, Frank," she murmured. "And I'm still grateful to you for that. Even though you weren't honest with our money, I know you'd be proud of the way our kids are pulling together to save this old place."

At that moment, Alexis stepped out of the kitchen, an affectionate smile on her face. She was wearing a big apron that was splashed with water and grease, and she looked very different from the fashionable, sad woman that Vivian had been seeing lately.

There was a hint of amusement in Alexis's eyes

as she grinned at her mother. "Talking to yourself, huh?"

Vivian smiled at her daughter. "I was getting a few things straight with Frank."

A sympathetic look appeared on Alexis's face and she nodded.

"Thanks for sticking around to help out so much, sweetheart." Vivian put an arm around her daughter and gave her a tight squeeze.

"It's my pleasure." Alexis laid her head down on her mother's shoulder. "I've been so wrapped up in my life in L.A. in recent years, and I think I kind of lost hold of who I am. It's been good to get back to my roots. And I've been worried about Grayson for so long—it's easier to put aside my worries about that here. It helps to be busy. I have next to nothing to do back there in our big mansion in L.A., and it's like I can't escape my fears there. Here, I get to keep my hands busy."

Vivian nodded sympathetically. "Always better to keep your hands busy."

"And planning this fundraiser has been especially helpful—it's been really keeping me occupied. After it ends and we save the pub, I don't know what I'm going to do. But I'll cross that bridge when I come to it."

Vivian looked into her daughter's eyes and brushed a strand of hair back from her forehead. "I'm so proud of you, Alexis. I know that whatever you do, you're going to be amazing at it."

Alexis inhaled and smiled at her mother. "Thanks, Mom. For what it's worth, I'm really proud of you too."

"Oh, it's worth a lot, honey."

They hugged again and then continued the work of closing up the pub for the night.

CHAPTER TWENTY-THREE

Julia strolled along the sidewalk of Rosewood Beach, grinning from ear to ear. It was a beautiful Monday morning, and the air was warmer and smelled sweeter than it had all spring. She was wearing a light blouse with jeans and comfortable heels, and she had done her makeup and hair carefully that morning. She was on her way to Greener Pastures, where Cooper worked.

I just know he's going to love this surprise, she thought, feeling as though she was about to burst with excitement. *This is the perfect way to thank him for all of the work he's been doing for my family.*

She practically skipped as she turned around a corner. She hadn't felt this excited in a long time, and she felt confident she was giving him the best surprise, and just the thing that he needed.

In her right hand was an envelope containing her gift to him, along with a paper bag containing Cooper's favorite boysenberry muffin from Seaside Sweets Bakery. In her left hand was an Americano for him, done up just the way she knew he liked it. She couldn't wait to see his face when she gave him all the things she'd picked out for him.

She reached Greener Pastures and stepped inside. A smiling receptionist gave her directions to Cooper's office, and she strode along the carpeted hallway toward it, her excitement growing.

The door to Cooper's office was ajar, and she peered through it. He was leaning back in his desk chair, talking on the phone, but the moment he saw her he sat straight up and started grinning.

"That sounds great. Tuesday it is," he said into the phone. "Looking forward to it. Bye." He hung up the phone and turned to Julia. "This is amazing! You're like a fairy, suddenly appearing. What's the occasion?"

He stood up and hurried over to her to give her a hug.

"Well, first of all, this coffee is for you." She set it

down proudly on his desk, excitement thrumming through her. "It should still be hot. And here is your favorite boysenberry muffin from Seaside Sweets Bakery."

"What?" He looked every bit as happy as she'd hoped he would, and her heart swelled with pleasure. "Julia, thank you. This is amazing. This is seriously so sweet of you."

"I'm so glad you like it." She grinned. "And I have so much more than treats for you." She held up the envelope triumphantly. "In here are tickets to the next Barn Rollers concert. One ticket for you, and one for me. You finally get to check that off your bucket list, and we get to do it together!"

"Oh my—what?" He grinned from ear to ear as he took the envelope from her and opened it. "I had no idea they were—" He stopped talking and his face fell when he looked at the tickets.

"What?" she asked, suddenly feeling worried. She didn't understand why he looked disappointed all of a sudden.

"I didn't realize... well, that city is five hours away from here. We'd have to stay overnight at a hotel."

"I know." She grinned again, relieved that she was about to take away his concern. "I already booked us a couple of hotel rooms. I've got the whole thing covered."

Cooper's lips parted, and she knew in the next instant that something was still wrong. Her heart sank. She'd expected him to be so happy, and he looked the opposite.

"I can't," he said, shaking his head. His voice was quiet. "I so wish I could—honestly, it sounds like a dream come true. It's so thoughtful of you. But I can't go."

"Why not?" she stammered, feeling confused and disappointed.

"I just can't leave Macey alone overnight. I don't feel comfortable leaving her with a sitter for that long. I've gotten more okay with leaving her for a few hours to go out in the evenings sometimes, but going away overnight feels like a lot. I'm not sure if Macey would be okay with that, and I'm not even sure I would be okay with it." He took a deep breath. "I'm sorry. I really am."

Julia shook her head. "No, there's no need to apologize. I should apologize—I clearly wasn't thinking." She felt terrible, as though she'd completely blundered. Her mind was racing, and she wondered if she knew how to date a single father after all. "I feel like I was totally inconsiderate—I didn't think it through like a parent would have."

"No, don't say that. The last thing I want is for you to feel bad about trying to do something so sweet for me. I'm sorry I can't go—I really am. I feel so rude for turning you down. I'm really touched by your thoughtfulness."

She shook her head. "I completely understand. There's nothing for you to feel bad about. I'm sorry for not checking with you first—it was silly to try to make it a surprise. I should have thought it all through better."

"No, if the surprise had worked out, it would have been perfect. I'm really grateful, Julia."

She smiled at him, but inside, her stomach was still sloshing with disappointment and embarrassment. "Well, at least you can still enjoy your coffee and your muffin." She laughed, doing her best to sound cheerful.

At that moment, his phone started to ring.

"I'll get out of your hair," she said, backing up toward the door and feeling glad of an excuse to leave. She felt so flustered that she needed some time to herself. "I'll see you next time we all get together to work on the fundraiser."

"Absolutely." He smiled at her, but his eyes looked sad. "Thank you again."

"Of course." She gave him the biggest smile she could muster, and then slipped out of the room.

She put on another smile as she passed the receptionist, who thankfully was also on the phone. Julia felt almost close to tears, and she didn't want to have to talk about what had just happened with anyone.

As she stepped out into the sunlight, she took a shaky breath. The exchange between herself and Cooper had rattled her badly—not only because she felt bad about not realizing that he wouldn't want to leave Macey alone all night, but also because it was making her question whether or not things could work out between them. She was afraid that she'd been wrong about the possibility of the two of them being good together.

I feel totally out of my depth when it comes to understanding what his life is like, she thought. *I'm not sure I'm ready to start acting like a co-parent.*

She swallowed, remembering the sad look he'd had in his eyes when she was leaving his office. He was probably questioning whether he'd really want to be with her or not.

The thought stung, but she couldn't brush it

aside. She felt sure that he must be starting to doubt their relationship, just like she was.

Wanting to distract herself, she started to walk in the direction of The Lighthouse Grill. There was always something to do there, and she wanted to help with something instead of continue to wrestle with her concerns alone.

CHAPTER TWENTY-FOUR

"Hey, Macey! Where's your other party shoe, honey?"

Cooper stuck his head out of Macey's closet. He felt silly for asking a two-year-old where her shoe was, but he was beginning to think she'd hidden it somewhere.

He glanced at his watch. The fundraiser would be starting in half an hour, and he was determined to not be late. He hadn't talked to Julia much since she'd bought him the tickets to the concert, and he was anxious to patch things up with her. He still felt terrible about the whole thing and hoped that it wouldn't cause her to lose interest in him. He felt worried that she thought he was boring and would never really be able to do anything fun with her if they continued to date.

"If I can't find this other shoe, she'll just have to wear tennis shoes with her dress," he muttered, sighing. Macey probably wouldn't care, she was only two—although he thought with a pang that his wife would have had her whole outfit ready to go the night before.

The doorbell rang, and he wiggled out of Macey's closet and hurried to answer it. Callie stood on the front doorstep, all smiles.

"Hey, Mr. Harris! How's it going?"

"Oh, fine." He smiled, trying not to appear too frazzled. "Thanks for agreeing to come with us to the fundraiser. It'll be a huge help."

"Oh, for sure. I know you need to be able to focus on the auction and things like that. Macey's going to have an amazing time, and we'll stay close enough that you'll be able to see us the whole time."

His smile became more genuine as he reflected how lucky he was to have found such a great babysitter. "Thanks, Callie. We'll be ready to go in just a minute here. I'm looking for Macey's other party shoe."

"Oh! I forgot to say something to you the other

day. I saw a shoe under the couch. A little black one, kind of shiny?"

"Oh, perfect." He heaved a sigh of relief. "I'll go check there."

He hurried to look under the couch, and Macey scampered up to Callie, looking excited. Sure enough, the shoe was under the couch, and in another couple of minutes, they were ready to go.

The plan was for the three of them to walk to the fundraiser together since the park where it was being held was only a short distance from Cooper's house. As soon as they started off along the sidewalk together, Macey slipped her hand into Callie's, seeming completely content and at-ease.

He watched the pair of them for a few moments, thinking to himself what good hands Macey was in when she was with Callie.

He thought again of Julia's gift to him with a pang. Maybe he'd been wrong to react the way that he had. He still didn't like the thought of staying away from his child overnight, but perhaps he'd panicked too much at the idea. After all, Macey usually went to sleep before he got back from his dates anyway. Would it matter so much if he returned home the next morning? She seemed completely comfortable with Callie, and he was learning how much he could trust the teenager to be responsible and make sure Macey felt okay.

He took a deep breath, feeling a knot in his stomach. He and Julia had barely spoken since the incident, and he guessed that she probably wasn't sure how to handle his abrupt rejection of her sweet gesture.

I handled it poorly, he thought regretfully, wanting to kick himself. *I shouldn't have turned her down so abruptly*.

"Look, Macey, there's the park," Callie said excitedly, pointing out the park up ahead as they walked. "That's where the fundraiser is! Like a giant party. Are you excited?"

"Yeah!" Macey looked up at Callie with an adoring, chubby smile, and Cooper felt his heart melt.

Suddenly, an idea struck him. His mind began to race, and he wondered if perhaps there was a way he could accept Julia's gift after all.

* * *

Alexis gazed around the fundraiser, feeling her heart swell with pride for her family. The park was packed with people, all of whom were smiling with enthusiasm and participating enthusiastically in all of the various games and activities.

She could see Vivian standing under a tree, talking to a couple of her life-long friends. Her mother's eyes were shining, and it was clear that the support of Rosewood Beach meant a great deal to her.

We're so lucky, Alexis thought. *People are really showing up for us and The Lighthouse Grill. This is going to change Mom's circumstances around.*

At his booth, Dean was showing kids how to put a toy engine back together like a puzzle. He was laughing and full of energy, and it warmed her heart to see him having a such a great time. Hazel and Jacob were manning the water games together, laughing and looking completely comfortable with each other.

It was a gorgeous, sunny day, and everyone seemed in high spirits. The grass of the park was lush and green, and pale green buds were beginning to unfurl on the branches of the trees. There seemed to be a spirit of excitement pervading the event that came from more than just people having fun. Everyone seemed to be aware that they were there for a shared purpose, and their joy was contagious and invigorating.

She'd been spending her day doing makeovers for a never-ending line of people and having an absolutely wonderful time. She loved seeing the looks of delight and surprise on her customers' faces when they saw their transformed appearances.

She felt her heart lift up with joy as her next customer approached. It was an elderly woman with short white hair, and Alexis immediately knew just what she wanted to do to make the woman feel more beautiful. She smiled, anticipating how happy the woman was going to feel, and then she was struck with a realization.

I might not be in L.A. living the life I thought I would be, she thought, *but my life has led me to being here, getting to do this in this moment. It's wonderful.*

She felt an almost bubbly kind of joy pass through her, and she told herself that she was done being idle. Whatever happened next, she was going to find something to work toward. She was going to move forward in her life with goals, and things to do.

She had almost finished giving the woman a makeover when she heard someone call out to her.

"Hey, sis!" Julia approached her booth, grinning. "How's it going here?"

"Amazingly." Alexis gestured to her current patron. "This beautiful woman here is my seventeenth customer. Doesn't she look amazing?"

The elderly woman laughed, looking pleased.

"Fantastic! You look beautiful, ma'am."

"Oh, tut," said the woman, laughing.

Alexis proclaimed the elderly woman all set, and she went on her way, looking thrilled. Julia lingered to talk to her sister, since for the first time that day, Alexis didn't have a customer in line for the makeover booth.

Julia's cheeks were flushed, and she looked starry-eyed with excitement. "We've already raised so much money from the auction items. Things are really going great."

Alexis reached over and squeezed her sister's hand, feeling a surge of relief. She'd believed that the fundraiser was going to work out, but it was nice to see that belief come true.

Out of the corner of her eye, she noticed Cooper talking to a couple of people at Dean's car repair booth. She turned back to Julia and saw that her sister was watching Cooper with a troubled expression on her face.

"You don't seem to be spending much time with Cooper today," Alexis said gently. "I thought you'd be practically glued to his arm, since Callie is here watching over Macey and he's free to be totally distracted by you."

Julia shrugged, but the gesture looked forced. "He's working on the fundraiser. He's busy talking to people."

Alexis gave her a look. "You can't fool me, missy. That's not really the reason."

Julia smiled a little at her sister's perceptiveness and sighed. "I think—" Her voice was soft. "I think I might have assumed too quickly that we could mesh our very different lifestyles together."

Alexis shook her head. "Don't give up yet. There's still so much to discover about each other. You don't know that it isn't going to work out. Besides," she added, glancing over at Cooper again and noticing that he was looking at her sister with a decidedly puppy-like expression, "it seems like Cooper is still very much interested in working things out. You shouldn't give up if he thinks things could work out between you two. Maybe they could."

She thought to herself with a pang of sadness that she wished that Grayson were trying harder to make things work out between the two of them, instead of being so silent and seemingly disinterested.

Julia smiled sadly, also glancing at Cooper for a moment. "Maybe you're right. But I don't know. I guess we'll just have to see." She lingered for a moment longer, as if she was lost in thought. Then she sighed. "Well, I better keep moving here. There's lots to be done."

"See you around." Alexis smiled and waved as Julia went off into the crowd. She noticed that her sister didn't head toward where Cooper was standing.

She sat quietly for a moment and then decided to stand up and stretch. She still didn't have anyone coming up to her booth for a makeover, so she thought to herself that she might walk over to where they were selling lemonade and cookies and get herself some refreshments.

As she was stepping away from her booth, her phone began to ring. Assuming it was one of her family members calling with a request or an update about the fundraiser, she pulled her cell phone from her pocket and was about to answer it when she read the name on the screen. It was Grayson.

Her heart did a somersault and she quickly answered the call.

"Hey, Grayson."

Her tongue felt heavy, and she realized that her heart was beating faster. She stepped away from the busyness of the fundraiser, heading toward a quiet patch of trees.

"Hey, sweetheart. I'm just checking in to say hello. I haven't heard from you in a while."

She blinked in surprise. She'd been trying so hard to not think about Grayson, feeling so perturbed over her fears that he was being unfaithful, that she hadn't texted him regularly like she used to. She hadn't meant to neglect to text him, it had happened by accident, but she never would have expected him to notice and call her about it.

"Oh, I've been so busy out here. We're having a fundraiser for the pub today. A big event in the middle of town, at the park. We've been planning it for days."

"A fundraiser?" He sounded surprised, and she wondered if he was taken back by the fact that she hadn't just asked him for the money. Her heart ached, wishing that things felt that easy between them.

"Yes, it was Julia's idea." She tried to sound breezy and cheerful. "It's been a lot of fun putting it together."

"Oh. Well. That's great, honey."

She winced. He almost sounded disappointed, as if he wished she'd told him more about it before it happened. She realized how much she was holding back from telling him, and she found herself longing for the honesty that had once existed between them.

"Grayson?" she asked softly.

"Yes?"

She took a deep breath, feeling her bloodstream rush faster. She was scared of what the answer to her question was going to be. "I—well, I was looking at our credit card statement and I saw that you've taken someone else out to eat a couple of times. I've been worried about it. I have to ask—are—are you seeing someone else?"

There were three full heartbeats of complete silence, and she felt as though the air around her was suddenly turning colder.

"You mean—another woman?" Grayson sounded completely shocked.

"Yes. You've been so distant lately, and I thought —well, I thought that maybe you..." Her voice trailed off.

"Alexis, I would never." He still sounded flabbergasted. "I did take someone out to dinner a couple of times, but it was this new client that I'm trying to close a deal with. And he's a pot-bellied, balding old man, for the record. Those were business meals. I would never cheat on you. Never."

Relief flooded her, and all at once she felt as light as a feather. "I don't mean to accuse you. I'm sorry I wasn't more trusting, but being away from home and dealing with everything surrounding Dad passing away has put me in a weird place. It's—well, it's been hard for me to trust you."

"I can understand that, and I'm sorry for it. I wish I'd done a better job of being there for you. I've been so busy—and the truth is I don't know how to comfort people who are grieving. I expected myself to mess it up, so I didn't try hard enough. I'm sorry."

"I forgive you." A kind of peace settled over her as she listened to his words. It wasn't just relief that he hadn't been unfaithful to her, it was more than that. A realization of what she needed to do for herself was growing in her, and she no longer felt as though he was the one who would decide whether she was happy in the future or not. She was realizing that no matter what happened, she was the person with that power.

Grayson, misinterpreting her pause, cleared his throat almost nervously. "Alexis, I promise nothing's been going on. Just work. If you want me to get you some kind of proof, I can—"

"No, I believe you." She smiled even though he couldn't see her. "But thanks for offering."

She looked out across the park at the fundraiser that her family had organized. Kids were whooping and running across the grass, and she saw so many people she knew and loved talking and laughing with each other. A sense of camaraderie, of love, seemed to be filling the event. There was a loyalty there in Rosewood Beach that she hadn't experienced in L.A., and she knew she wanted to stay in her hometown longer. She wanted to stay with her siblings as they worked together to help their mom get the pub back on its feet.

"The truth is that I've been making a decision while we've been talking," she said softly.

There was a slight pause, and then Grayson asked slowly, "What is it?"

"I think it's best that I spend some more time here with my family for the time being. I want to extend my time in Rosewood."

"Okay. That's good, honey. I think you should do that."

She blinked, almost feeling stung by his reaction. She didn't know how she'd expected him to react, but the fact that he didn't seem disappointed by her decision made her feel insecure. She wished he'd at least hinted that he was hoping she'd come back soon.

"I—I hope that's all right," she said, a little stiffly.

"Absolutely. You do what you need to do." His response sounded a little stiff as well, and her heart ached for a moment as she wondered what he was really thinking. Was he just trying to be supportive, or did he truly not care if she came back yet or not? She wished that he needed her, and she wished that she knew what to say to get them back to a better place.

Maybe he's feeling the same way, she thought, thinking about how he'd said he didn't know how to help her with her grief, so he hadn't stepped up to support her. *Maybe he just has no idea what to say, so he isn't saying anything.*

"Well, we should talk again soon," she said, noticing Julia waving to her. Her sister had a huge smile on her face, and she guessed that something exciting had happened at the fundraiser. "I'd better get back to my booth here."

"Yes, we should talk again soon. Have a good rest of your day, sweetheart."

"You too."

"Bye, honey."

"Bye."

She hung up the phone, smiling quietly to herself. She still felt uncertain about what the future was going to hold, but she felt at peace with her decision. For now, she was going to stay in Rosewood Beach with her family, and work to keep The Lighthouse Grill on its feet. She tucked her phone in her pocket and hurried over to talk to Julia.

CHAPTER TWENTY-FIVE

Cooper leaned back in the booth and smiled across the table at Julia. He felt tired but incredibly content. Beside him, Dean was excitedly reading off the list of all of the money they'd raised at the fundraiser that day.

"There," Dean said with a sigh, coming to the end of the list. "That's definitely enough to keep The Lighthouse Grill on its feet for now. I'm so proud of you chuckleheads."

"This is amazing." Alexis's eyes were shining. "We really did it. Our fundraiser was a success."

Julia nodded and smiled, taking a sip of her root beer float. After the fundraiser had ended, Vivian, the Owens siblings, and Cooper had gone over to the pub for celebratory sandwiches and root beer floats.

Callie had taken Macey home to go to sleep, and Cooper felt grateful that he was able to stay with Julia and her family. He still wanted a chance to talk with her about the two of them, and what had happened the other day.

"It was wildly successful." Vivian beamed at her children, and tears glistened in her eyes. "I'm so thankful for all of you, and the hard work you put into this fundraiser. Thank you. Thank you so much." She looked at Cooper, and he smiled back at her.

"Of course, Mom." Hazel wrapped an arm around her mother and hugged her sideways. "We love you and the pub. We had to put up a good fight."

"And it sounds like we won that fight." Julia clasped her hands together. "We don't have enough money to make the pub's finances carefree forever, but we definitely have enough to fill in the gaps of uncertainty that Dad left."

"Thank goodness." Hazel let out a long sigh. "I'm exhausted, but I feel so happy."

"Me too." Alexis smiled, and Julia leaned her head down onto her sister's shoulder.

"I feel almost overwhelmed with happiness," Vivian said, clasping her hands. "I'm so grateful to you all. Thank you for having this idea and for working so hard to put it into action."

"Of course, Mom." Julia looked lovingly at her mother. "We're here to support you and make sure that you don't need endless security for the pub. I'm going to make sure you have what you need."

"Me too," Alexis said. "You can count on it."

"And me," said Dean, nodding. "We've got your back, Mom."

"Yes, we do." Hazel smiled at her mother. "No matter what happens, you've got us to look out for you."

Cooper felt his heart stir with happiness as he listened to the Owens siblings offer their support to their mother. He felt touched by how much their family loved each other, and he felt confident that they were going to succeed in keeping the pub afloat.

"Yes, you do." Julia nodded emphatically. "We're all going to help out however we can to sustain the pub's legacy."

"That's right," said Dean. "The dream you and Dad built together is worth preserving."

Vivian's eyes filled with tears and she placed her hands on her heart. "This place belongs to our family. I'm so glad you children care about it as much as I do."

Cooper watched Julia smiling at her mother and he tried to catch her eye. She didn't look in his direction, and his heart sank a little. It seemed as though she was always looking away whenever he glanced at her, and he felt as though that was evidence that she still felt awkward about the gift that he'd rejected. He wished that she was trying to catch his eye like he was trying to catch hers, and showing the same interest in him that she had in the past.

He was just getting ready to clear his throat and ask her what her next plans for the pub were, when the front door of The Lighthouse Grill opened and someone stepped inside.

"Well, well, well." Dean eyed the person darkly. "Look who it is."

Cooper turned his head curiously and saw that the person was none other than Judd McCormick.

Judd strolled up to the booth where they were sitting, looking as poised and confident as a peacock. "Good evening, folks." He smiled his flashy, insincere smile. "I heard about your fundraiser today. I just happened to be passing by, and I thought I'd drop in and offer my congratulations."

Cooper's eyes narrowed at the other man. He

had a feeling that Judd had in fact not been passing by but had driven over to the pub on purpose.

"Well, that's nice of you, Mr. McCormick," Vivian said, politely but coolly.

Dean, clearly less inclined to be gracious, cleared his throat loudly and glared at Judd as if telling him that his congratulations weren't welcome.

"How much money were you able to raise?" Judd smiled, but his eyes glittered calculatingly. "I know not a lot of people in this town have much extra money."

"We raised a great deal." Julia's smile was hard, and the look in her eyes was almost aggressive.

"Really now?" Judd's eyebrows lifted in surprise for a moment, but then his smile returned and he seemed unfazed. "Well, Vivian, you're lucky you have such great helpers in the form of your kids. I'm sure what they've done today is going to get you through the next few weeks and maybe even the next few months, but when you find yourself in financial trouble again, feel free to give me a call."

"Now why on earth would I do that?" Vivian said. The look in her eyes was starting to look similar to the one in Julia's.

Judd shrugged. "I hate to say it, but once your

kids go their separate ways again, I think you're going to find yourself with the same issues as before."

Vivian squared her shoulders. "That's none of your business, Judd. And furthermore, you're wrong. That won't be a problem. My kids aren't going to be leaving me to fend for myself. We are family, and we've all agreed to do whatever we need to do to preserve the pub."

Judd's eyes narrowed. "Well, if you ever find yourself reconsidering my offer—"

"No, Judd." Cooper spoke up, looking the other man square in the eyes. "You're the one who needs to reconsider your offer. I've worked out some of the landscaping details, and I don't think the pub would be a good spot for the McCormick expansion. You'd be better off buying more square footage somewhere else—somewhere else that doesn't involve destroying a restaurant that serves as a center of community in this town."

"I—well—" Judd stammered, seeming to be at a loss for words.

Cooper found himself glancing at Julia, and his heart swelled when he saw that she was looking at him with a glow in her eyes.

"That's my professional opinion," Cooper said. "Honestly. And my personal opinion is that you should have learned your lesson by now. The location isn't what makes this pub popular. It's the food and the atmosphere and the people who run it. You can't buy that. Take a hint from the way the fundraiser went today. The people of Rosewood Beach love The Lighthouse Grill. If you take it away from them, they're going to want nothing to do with your brewery."

Judd blinked. For a moment, he hesitated, as if he was trying to think of something to say. Then he swallowed, turned around, and left the pub.

"Three cheers for Cooper!" Dean laughed.

"I have a very good feeling that this time, he's actually leaving for good." Vivian was all smiles.

"I propose a toast," Alexis said, lifting her glass of wine. "To The Lighthouse Grill."

"To The Lighthouse Grill," Julia echoed, holding her root beer float aloft. "May it have a long and prosperous future."

They all clinked their glasses together, laughing and cheering.

"I have no doubt it will." Vivian smiled. "Frank would have been so proud of you all today. So proud."

They continued to talk and laugh as they finished their drinks and their sandwiches. Everyone seemed to be in holiday spirits, and a sense of relief and celebration pervaded the rest of the meal.

As everyone else lingered at the table to talk and sip what remained of their drinks, Julia stood up and picked up a few of the empty plates. She headed into the kitchen alone with the dishes, and after hesitating for a moment, Cooper stood up as well. He took a couple more empty plates and followed her into the kitchen. He was hoping to be able to catch a moment alone with her so that they could discuss what had happened between them the other day.

He pushed open the swinging doors of the kitchen with his elbow and saw Julia setting her dishes down next to a large sink. One of the cooks was bustling away at the stove, humming to herself as she cooked, and listening to unheard music on a pair of earbuds.

"Hey," he said to Julia, almost breathlessly. "Do you have a second?"

Julia turned around hurriedly and pressed her lips together. She looked suddenly nervous, and for a moment he was worried that she was going to make an excuse and leave the kitchen without talking to him.

"Yeah." She smiled almost shyly at him, and he

noted that he still got swarms of butterflies in his chest when he was close to her.

"I want to discuss those tickets you offered, if that's all right."

Julia nodded slowly. "I expected you to still be thinking about that whole thing. I know I am. I think I was too hasty and I should have given it all more thought. I can't expect you to change your whole way of life around for me. I know you're a great father, and you take parenting seriously. Honestly I feel so embarrassed about the whole thing."

He stepped up to her and took her hands. "No, Julia." She squeezed his hands back gently, and he felt his heart rate pick up. "You shouldn't feel embarrassed. This is new territory for both of us, and we just need to compromise to make this work. Our different ways of living don't need to stop us from going out together; we just need to figure out how to adapt."

She nodded, and there was a hopeful look in her eyes that hadn't been there a moment before.

"And besides," he continued, starting to smile, "I had a thought. I could ask Callie to come along on the day of the concert to watch Macey. She could sleep in your hotel room with you, and Macey could spend the night with me. It wouldn't be exactly what you were thinking, but we would still have our time together and get to go to the concert together. And I would be doing what I need to do to feel as though I'm taking good care of Macey."

He saw tears spring into Julia's eyes, and she nodded. "That's a great idea. A really great idea." She smiled at him and laughed breathlessly. "I wish I'd thought of that. I'm sorry I didn't."

"You stop apologizing there, missy." He grinned at her. "Besides, I feel as though I completely messed that whole thing up by reacting the way I did. We'll be learning together."

His eyes traced over her face for a few heartbeats, and then the words that had been beating around in his chest for a while spilled out of him.

"I've never really been interested in being more than a single dad. Ever since Macey's mom died, I haven't felt any interest in dating anyone, even though raising Macey alone has been hard. But... well, I like you a lot, Julia Owens. So if you're willing to stumble around with me in the dark while we figure out how to do this, I'm game if you are. I want to see where things could go between us, because I think it could be pretty amazing."

She took a deep breath, looking serious. For a moment, his heart skipped a beat as he wondered if she was about to tell him that she didn't think things could work out between them. Then she grinned at him and nodded.

"I really like that plan, Mr. Harris," she said.

His heart leapt up in happiness, and he was suddenly filled with excitement for the days ahead.

"I'm so glad you said that," he murmured. "Me too."

And with that, he drew her in for a kiss.

CHAPTER TWENTY-SIX

Julia looked over at Cooper and found herself grinning from ear to ear. He was staring up at the stage where the Barn Rollers were performing with a completely enraptured expression.

He's adorable, she thought, feeling a rush of fondness for him. *I'm so glad everything worked out, and he was able to come to this concert with me.*

She turned back to the stage, swaying a little to the rollicking beat. Cooper had been right when he'd said that she would have a new appreciation for country music if she got a chance to go to a live country music concert. The concert hall was filled with a positive energy as people cheered and danced and sang along to the music.

She glanced at Cooper again, thinking to herself

that she was enjoying watching him as much as she was enjoying watching the concert itself. He was so into it, and she couldn't help smiling again as she watched him nod along to the songs and mouth all the words. After a few seconds, he glanced at her and grinned.

"Are you enjoying it?" he shouted above the noise.

"Yes!" She slipped her hand inside his, and he swayed back and forth a few times playfully, causing her to sway with him.

They continued to have a wonderful time together for the remainder of the concert. After the band left the stage, the audience cheered so loudly and for so long that there was an encore performance. Julia found herself tapping her foot and clapping her hands just as enthusiastically as all the people around her as the concert officially ended.

"Wow, that was amazing." Cooper couldn't seem to stop grinning as they moved along with the crowd toward the exits. "I mean seriously, that was so good. They're so good. And it was so awesome to see them live like that. The music was just—I don't know, I just got totally swept away by it."

She couldn't help laughing, he was so charming.

"What?" he asked, smiling at her as they stepped

out of the concert hall onto the sidewalk. The crowd thinned out as people went off in separate directions, and the sounds of the city purred in the background. Streetlights cast a warm glow over everything, and neon lights blossomed like strange electric flowers in the distance.

"Are you glad we went?" she teased, and he stopped walking and pulled her into his arms.

"I'm so glad." His eyes were shining at her. "Thank you so much for thinking of this and making it happen."

"Thank you for coming with me, and for figuring out how to make it work. I know what a big deal it was for you to do this, bringing Macey to the city and organizing having Callie come along with us. I know it was a lot of work for you, and you had to pay Callie to be here—"

He brushed her hair behind her ear, looking into her eyes fondly. "You're worth it."

Her stomach fluttered with happiness, and he drew her in for a kiss, which made her feel as though she was on top of the world.

They walked slowly to the garage where they'd parked Cooper's car, and from there drove back to the hotel. They talked excitedly about the concert together the whole way.

"Let's go talk to Callie together," Cooper said as they stepped inside the hotel's elevator. "I don't want to say goodnight yet, but I do want to check on Macey right away."

"Sure." She smiled at him.

They went to Cooper's room, where Callie had been watching Macey. As they tiptoed inside, they saw Macey sound asleep in one of the beds, holding a stuffed panda toy tightly. Callie was sitting by the window reading a book under a lamp, and she had the overhead lights dimmed to make it easier for Macey to sleep.

"Hey, you guys." Callie spoke in a whisper, but she grinned and stood up as soon as they stepped inside the room. "How was the concert?"

"Amazing," Cooper whispered, grinning as well. "How did everything go here?"

"Great. There was a moment when she was starting to get fussy, but we played some games and then watched a movie. Then I read her a couple of books and she went right to sleep." As she talked, Callie looked both at Cooper and at Julia, clearly including Julia in the report. Julia felt a little strange about it, but at the same time, it meant a lot to her.

"Fantastic. Thank you so much." Cooper smiled at the teenager. "I'm glad you both had a good night."

Callie nodded. "And speaking of goodnight, I'll head on over to our room, Julia. All that reading has made me pretty sleepy too." She laughed.

Callie slipped out of the hotel room and Cooper turned to Julia with a smile.

"Thank you again. Tonight has been amazing."

"You're so welcome."

They shared another kiss, and then wished each other goodnight in whispers as Julia quietly left the room.

She walked slowly along the hallway of the hotel, unable to stop herself from smiling as butterflies flapped in her stomach.

"Good morning, Daddy!"

Cooper opened his eyes and saw Macey sitting up in her bed, looking over at him with a big smile on her face. Sunlight was streaming in through the windows of their hotel room, and he smiled to himself, realizing that this was one of the first nights in a long time that Macey had slept the whole night without waking him up. Kind of ironic, he thought, but he was thrilled.

"Good morning, honey." He climbed out of bed

and went to give her a hug and a kiss. "Callie said you guys had a great time last night."

"Yeah! Can we come back here soon?"

He chuckled. Macey had been having a wonderful time, clearly considering the trip to be some kind of amazing adventure. She'd been happy and excited the day before, and he was glad to see that she still felt that way that morning.

Half an hour later, as he was putting on her shoes, she said, "Can we get breakfast with Julia?"

He grinned, delighted that she wanted to spend time with Julia. "I think that sounds like a great idea. Should we go ask Julia if she wants to?"

"Yeah!" She wiggled off the chair she was sitting on and toddled toward the door of their room.

They made their way over to Julia and Callie's room and knocked on the door. A moment later, Julia, wearing a yellow sundress and smiling broadly, opened the door.

"Good morning!" She crouched down to be on Macey's level. "How are you this morning, Miss Macey?"

"I'm hungry," Macey said. "Do you want to get breakfast with us?"

Julia grinned at the little girl. "I would love to."

"You're invited too, Callie," Cooper called into

the hotel room. "Do you want to come get breakfast with us?"

"No, thanks for the invitation, but I think I'm going to order something from the hotel and watch cartoons." Callie, who was still wearing her pajamas, waved at them. "But you guys have fun!"

Julia grabbed her purse and tugged on a pair of sandals, and then she proclaimed herself ready to go. The three of them took the elevator downstairs, where they asked the receptionist for restaurant recommendations. She suggested a place that was a short walk from the hotel, and they began to make their way there, with Cooper holding Macey in his arms.

The restaurant was charming, and they got a booth in the back which offered a beautiful view of the ocean. Cooper ordered chocolate chip pancakes for himself and Macey, and Julia ordered a yogurt parfait with sides of scrambled eggs and hash browns. Macey babbled excitedly throughout their meal, asking questions about the concert.

"Was it loud?" Macey asked, wiggling excitedly in her seat as Cooper cut up her pancakes into lots of little pieces.

"Yes, but in a fun way." Julia grinned at her, and Cooper's heart warmed with happiness to see the way Macey looked at Julia. She seemed to really love her.

"I'd like to make a toast," Cooper said, raising his cup of coffee. "To today—the first of many."

He made eye contact with Julia, smiling. He was implying that there would be many more times that he and Julia went out together, and that there would be many more times that the three of them spent time together.

Julia flushed, and Cooper loved the way she smiled at his words.

I mean it, he thought, telling himself that he was going to say as much to her later when they had a moment alone together. *I want many more mornings just like this one, with these two.*

"To the first of many," Julia echoed softly, and she and Cooper shared a warm smile across the table. His heartbeat quickened with happiness as he let himself picture what their future might look like.

CHAPTER TWENTY-SEVEN

A month later, Julia and Macey were at the park with Hazel and Samantha, enjoying the warm weather and the golden sunshine.

"It's such a nice day, isn't it?" Hazel leaned back against the bench that she and Julia were sitting on, letting out a luxurious sigh. "This breeze off the ocean is delicious. And look at those two."

"I know." Julia grinned as she watched Samantha play with Macey on the playground. The older girl was taking special care of the toddler, and both of them were clearly having a wonderful time. "I was planning on bringing Macey over to Cooper's office when he finishes work, but I might ask him to meet us here. I think he'd love to be out in the sunshine for a while."

"Careful, Macey!" Samantha said, following the little girl up the playground steps. "You can sit on my lap while we go down the slide." She looked up at her mother and aunt and mouthed, *she's so cute.*

Julia laughed and called out, "You both are!"

Samantha bowed and settled Macey on her lap before carefully going down the slide.

"Samantha loves being around her," Hazel said, watching them fondly. "She really has a knack for taking care of kids."

"Perfect, sounds like Cooper will have a babysitter backup when Callie goes off to college." Julia chuckled.

"Yeah, and he might have you as backup too." Hazel grinned at her. "Sounds like things are going very well between the two of you."

"They are." Julia let out a happy sigh. "He's—well, he's just amazing. I feel like I like him better and better every time I see him. Ever since we had so much fun at the concert together, it's like we've reached a new level in our relationship. We're learning a lot about each other and how to manage having Macey be a part of our relationship."

"Are you officially official yet?" Hazel asked, clapping her hands.

"I guess that depends on how you define official."

Julia laughed. "We haven't decided on anything solid yet, we just know that we definitely want to keep getting to know each other and seeing how this can work out." Her heart felt light as she contemplated the future.

"Mmm. But you're smitten, clearly."

"Okay, enough about me! Have you talked to Jacob since the fundraiser?"

"No," Hazel said, flushing bright pink immediately. "I've thought about reaching out once or twice, but I don't know; he's so busy."

"Girl, come on, you've got to make a move," Julia teased, grinning at her sister.

Hazel blushed a deeper shade of pink and brushed her hand through the air, dismissing Julia's comment. "I'm okay. I don't really know that I'm up for trying to date again, if I'm being honest."

Julia nodded, smiling at her sister, but her heart twisted a little in sympathy. She guessed that Hazel was scared to make a move, because it had been such a long time since she'd been in the dating scene. "I know it can all seem scary, but I think making an attempt would be worth it."

Hazel bit her lip. "I'm not sure I'm ready to take that leap and face the possibility of rejection." She let out a long sigh, and Julia wondered if she was thinking about how long she'd had a crush on Jacob. "But I'm glad things are going well for you!" Hazel's brisk tone made it clear that she was cheerfully trying to change the subject. "You're doing so great with Macey. It's not easy to get used to caring for little kids, but you really seem to have gotten the hang of it."

"Oh, that's sweet of you to say. I do feel like I know what I'm doing now—well, for the most part." She laughed. "And I have to admit, it's been a lot of fun. She's such a sweetheart, and she says the funniest things sometimes."

She watched Macey as she spoke, feeling a surge of fondness for the little girl. She could hardly believe that she'd grown so used to having Macey around. The relationship between the two of them was different than what she'd expected, and it was wonderful.

At that moment, her phone buzzed with a text from Cooper. She started to read it eagerly, and Hazel laughed.

"Ooh, a text from the man! What does he say?"

Julia finished reading the text before answering. "Well, there's a bit of a hiccup. He says he has to go and check out a job last minute, so he said we should head home instead of meeting him in town like we'd planned. But then he suggests that instead of eating dinner at his place, we get a sitter for Macey so he can take me out for a romantic evening."

"Aww, that's sweet! It sounds like Cooper is getting more flexible and comfortable in your relationship too. He's learning how to balance dating with being a single father."

Julia nodded, happily. "I think so too."

"And Samantha and I would be happy to watch Macey tonight. We'll make some mac and cheese and watch kiddie movies. It'll be a party."

"Thank you!" Julia reached over and gave her sister a hug. "She always has a great time with you guys."

"We love it when she visits."

Julia grinned at her sister and then turned back to her phone to text Cooper. Her heart felt light as she typed the words, and the warm spring breeze ruffled her hair.

JULIA: We're on.

ALSO BY FIONA BAKER

The Marigold Island Series

The Beachside Inn

Beachside Beginnings

Beachside Promises

Beachside Secrets

Beachside Memories

Beachside Weddings

Beachside Holidays

Beachside Treasures

The Sea Breeze Cove Series

The House by the Shore

A Season of Second Chances

A Secret in the Tides

The Promise of Forever

A Haven in the Cove

The Blessing of Tomorrow

A Memory of Moonlight

The Saltwater Sunsets Series

Whale Harbor Dreams

Whale Harbor Sisters

Whale Harbor Reunions

Whale Harbor Horizons

Whale Harbor Vows

Whale Harbor Blooms

Whale Harbor Adventures

Whale Harbor Blessings

The Rosewood Beach Series

Return to Rosewood Beach

Sea Glass Serenade

A Place for Daydreams

A Bright Winter Season

Moonlit Harbor Nights

Where Sea Meets Sky

A New Chapter in Rosewood Beach

Wishes at Water's Edge

A Breeze over Rosewood Beach

Under the Lighthouse Glow

Autumn by the Seashore

Footsteps in the Sand

Evergreen Hollow Christmas

The Inn at Evergreen Hollow

Snowflakes and Surprises

A Christmas to Remember

Mistletoe and Memories

A Season of Magic

The Snowy Pine Ridge Series

The Christmas Lodge

Sweet Christmas Wish

Second Chance Christmas

Christmas at the Guest House

A Cozy Christmas Escape

The Christmas Reunion

**For a full list of my books and series, visit my
website at** www.fionabakerauthor.com!

ABOUT THE AUTHOR

Fiona writes sweet, feel-good contemporary women's fiction and family sagas with a bit of romance.

She hopes her characters will start to feel like old friends as you follow them on their journeys of love, family, friendship, and new beginnings. Her heartwarming storylines and charming small-town beach settings are a particular favorite of readers.

When she's not writing, she loves eating good meals with friends, trying out new recipes, and finding the perfect glass of wine to pair them with. She lives on the East Coast with her husband and their two trouble-making dogs.

Follow her on her website, Facebook, or Bookbub.

Sign up to receive her newsletter, where you'll get free books, exclusive bonus content, and info on her new releases and sales!

Made in the USA
Columbia, SC
05 February 2025

53341614R00193